Charmed By You

Also From J. Kenner

Fallen Saint Series:
My Fallen Saint
My Beautiful Sin
My Cruel Salvation
Sinner's Game

Stark Security:
Shattered With You
Broken With You
Ruined With You
Wrecked With You
Destroyed With You
Memories of You
Ravaged With You
Hidden With You
Charmed By You

The Stark Saga:
Release Me
Claim Me
Complete Me
Anchor Me
Lost With Me
Damien
Enchant Me
Interview With The Billionaire

Stark Ever After:
Take Me
Have Me
Play My Game
Seduce Me
Unwrap Me
Deepest Kiss
Entice Me
Hold Me
Please Me

Indulge Me
Delight Me
Cherish Me
Embrace Me

Stark International
Steele Trilogy:
Say My Name
On My Knees
Under My Skin
Take My Dare (novella, includes bonus short story: Steal My Heart)

Stark World Standalone Stories:
Justify Me **(part of the Lexi Blake Crossover Collection)**

Jamie & Ryan Novellas:
Tame Me
Tempt Me
Tease Me

Dallas & Jane (S.I.N. Trilogy):
Dirtiest Secret
Hottest Mess
Sweetest Taboo

Most Wanted:
Wanted
Heated
Ignited

Wicked Nights:
Wicked Grind
Wicked Dirty
Wicked Torture

Man of the Month:
Down On Me
Hold On Tight
Need You Now
Start Me Up

Get It On
In Your Eyes
Turn Me On
Shake It Up
All Night Long
In Too Deep
Light My Fire
Walk The Line
Royal Cocktail
Bar Bites: A Man of the Month Cookbook

Blackwell-Lyon:
Lovely Little Liar
Pretty Little Player
Sexy Little Sinner
Tempting Little Tease

Also by Julie Kenner

Demon Hunting Soccer Mom Series:
Carpe Demon
California Demon
Demons Are Forever
Deja Demon
The Demon You Know
Demon Ex Machina
Pax Demonica
Day of the Demon
How to Train Your Demon

The Dark Pleasures Series:
Caress of Darkness
Find Me in Darkness
Find Me in Pleasure
Find Me in Passion
Caress of Pleasure

Rising Storm:
Tempest Rising
Quiet Storm

Charmed By You

A Stark Security Novella
By J. Kenner

1001 DARK NIGHTS
PRESS

Charmed By You
A Stark Security Novella
By J. Kenner

Copyright 2022 Julie Kenner
ISBN: 978-1-951812-92-8

Foreword: Copyright 2014 M. J. Rose

Published by 1001 Dark Nights Press, an imprint of Evil Eye Concepts,
Incorporated

Sign up for the 1001 Dark Nights Newsletter
and be entered to win a Tiffany Key necklace.

There's a contest every month!

Go to www.1001DarkNights.com to subscribe.

As a bonus, all subscribers can download
FIVE FREE exclusive books!

Acknowledgments from the Author

Huge hugs to Liz, MJ, Jillian, Kim, and the whole team at 1001! And, of course, to Stark fans everywhere; you all are the best!

One Thousand and One Dark Nights

Once upon a time, in the future…

*I was a student fascinated with stories and learning.
I studied philosophy, poetry, history, the occult, and
the art and science of love and magic. I had a vast
library at my father's home and collected thousands
of volumes of fantastic tales.*

*I learned all about ancient races and bygone
times. About myths and legends and dreams of all
people through the millennium. And the more I read
the stronger my imagination grew until I discovered
that I was able to travel into the stories… to actually
become part of them.*

*I wish I could say that I listened to my teacher
and respected my gift, as I ought to have. If I had, I
would not be telling you this tale now.
But I was foolhardy and confused, showing off
with bravery.*

*One afternoon, curious about the myth of the
Arabian Nights, I traveled back to ancient Persia to
see for myself if it was true that every day Shahryar
(Persian: شهریار, "king") married a new virgin, and then
sent yesterday's wife to be beheaded. It was written
and I had read that by the time he met Scheherazade,
the vizier's daughter, he'd killed one thousand
women.*

*Something went wrong with my efforts. I arrived
in the midst of the story and somehow exchanged
places with Scheherazade — a phenomena that had
never occurred before and that still to this day, I
cannot explain.*

*Now I am trapped in that ancient past. I have
taken on Scheherazade's life and the only way I can
protect myself and stay alive is to do what she did to
protect herself and stay alive.*

*Every night the King calls for me and listens as I spin tales.
And when the evening ends and dawn breaks, I stop at a
point that leaves him breathless and yearning for more.
And so the King spares my life for one more day, so that
he might hear the rest of my dark tale.*

*As soon as I finish a story... I begin a new
one... like the one that you, dear reader, have before
you now.*

Prologue

I never believed in love. Why would I when the only love I ever saw was pretend?

I'd watched my parents pretending, and I'd known it wasn't real.

I stood under hot lights in front of a camera, faking emotions from the time I was five.

I screamed in fury, kissed with passion, and burned with the need for revenge.

I loved deeply. Rapturously.

Jealously flowed through my veins along with need and longing and violent lust.

But it was never real. Not under those lights with the cameras running and the crew standing silently nearby.

And certainly not in the world outside the sound stage where I drew men close, wanting to lose myself in the forgetfulness of lust and passion, but never wanting them to know me, much less love me.

I was hollow. Alone.

Then he came along, all strength and icy determination. As bold and brash as a leading man. He promised to keep me safe. And though there's no denying the attraction between us, he told me to keep my distance.

I tell myself I don't want him.

I know that I can't love him.

But, oh, how I wish that I could.

Chapter One

Get a grip, Frannie. You've got this.

I stand in my kitchen and draw in a breath, determined to listen to my own pep talk. Yes, it's a threat. But that doesn't mean I have to be scared.

And even if I am scared, that doesn't mean I have to show it.

I'm a good actress, after all. I know this. Hell, everyone knows it. I've been in front of the camera my whole life—literally. My little tush was filmed on many a changing table for diaper commercials, and I was the baby or toddler in so many *Law & Order*-type shows I can't even remember them all.

Granted, that was more like modeling, not acting. But I've been doing the real thing—stepping into another persona, acting the part— since I was six and landed my first soap opera. At nine, my character died in a tragic helicopter crash, but that was okay. I'd been noticed, and after that, I'd played the perky elementary-age daughter in many a big-screen rom com, then the best friend, then the love interest.

And, of course, there's *Bright Eyes*, the family sitcom that centered around the Bright family with the single dad and seven darling kids who were more than a handful. I was ten when I landed the role of Kelly Bright, the second youngest daughter. That show ran for a decade, and even though so much of it was hell, the bottom line is that I kicked serious acting ass, even parlaying that part into bigger movie roles.

Basically, I worked my tail off. I listened to my directors, took classes, and honed my craft. I've won Emmys and Academy Awards and raves from critics all over the globe.

Bottom line? I know how to act. More important, I know how to fake it.

And yet here I am standing in my very own house with absolutely no idea of the part I should be playing.

I draw a deep breath, then look around the kitchen. I'd supposedly come in here to top off my orange juice, but that had just been the best excuse I could come up with in the moment.

The real reason was to get away from the cabal forming in my dining area—the slew of friends and security specialists sitting around my dining table as they bang out ideas for how to keep me alive.

Alive.

Someone is trying to kill me, and the blow or the bullet or the poison or whatever could come from anywhere at any time. I'll have no warning. No control. And that team in there is supposed to protect me, but I'm not running that show either. They're just taking over, doing all the things to keep me safe. To keep me managed.

I shudder, but whether it's because of fear from the cryptic note or the hard memory of my father's controlling hand, I really don't know. I gasp, suddenly lost in the past, and the glass I'm holding slips through my fingers and breaks on the Italian marble floor.

I gape at the mess of glass and OJ at my feet, then jump when one of the Stark Security guys bursts through the door. He's tall and muscular, with thick honey-blond hair and green eyes with the kind of glorious lashes I pay a small fortune for. I can't recall his name, though it's on the tip of my tongue.

He's not as hot as some of the men I've been cast opposite, but I wouldn't kick him out of my bed. Of course, as far as every ridiculous tabloid-style website is concerned, I never kick anyone out of my bed.

"Careful," I say, nodding to the mess. "The tiles are slippery when they get wet."

"Especially in those shoes," he says, glancing at my feet. I'm wearing silk slacks, a tank, and a matching jacket. A semi-casual power outfit designed to convey that I'm in charge. And, naturally, I've paired it with my favorite heels. I look elegant and in control.

Unfortunately, he's absolutely right. Slip on the OJ, and I'll look like a fool, not like a confident woman who's taking control of a bad situation by hiring a bodyguard.

"Did you need something?" I ask.

His brows rise with what I can only assume is surprise. "I heard the glass break. I came to check on you."

"You can see that I'm fine," I snap, then immediately want to kick myself. I wish I could take back the words. At the very least, I should apologize for the tone. But I don't. I have a reputation for being strong and in control. I drive hard bargains in my movie deals, and publicists know better than to try to push me around. Maybe I do need a bodyguard—but I do *not* need to lose control of the situation or show anyone that I'm scared.

I lift my chin, making sure my fear and embarrassment are hidden. That much, at least, is easy. I'm an actress, after all. "You can go," I say. "I'll just put a towel over it. Deb can clean it later," I add, referring to my housekeeper.

He doesn't go, and I'm about to order him out when he takes one long stride toward me.

"You shouldn't be in here at all. You said you were going into the staging area. Not the kitchen." His voice is hard and harsh, and I recoil from this unexpected intensity.

"There wasn't anything to drink in the staging area's fridge," I explain. "So I headed the rest of the way into the kitchen. It's hardly like I breached the Pentagon."

The swinging doors off the dining area enter into a small corridor where staff can keep drinks, extra napkins, appetizers under warmers, and all the other necessities that make a formal dinner party flow smoothly. That staging area is like a short hallway, with another set of swinging doors that open onto the massive, commercial quality kitchen, which is where we are now. This room is huge and airy, with a massive granite island and walls of picture windows that look out over the property. And that, of course, is the problem. Which I know. But which I wasn't thinking about because all I wanted was an excuse to leave that table before I broke down and revealed to the entire team how scared I truly am.

He rubs his temples and sighs. "I thought you understood. The team is upgrading your security system right now," he continues. "That means it's partially off. That means that anyone could have slipped onto the property, lifted a gun, and shot you through that window."

"But they didn't." The moment I say the words, I realize how idiotic they sound. I know I should call them back, but that would be admitting that I screwed up. That I lost control of the situation.

"Is that really the argument you want to make to justify your behavior?" His voice is tight, and when he speaks, it's as if he's talking to a naughty five-year-old. I might have been scared and contrite a few moments ago, but now I'm just pissed. "Who the hell do you think you are?"

"The man assigned to keep you alive," he says at the same moment I remember his name.

"Mr. Barré," I say. His name is Simon Barré. I make a show of looking him up and down. He and all the others might be in my house because I'm scared for my safety, but there is no way I'm going to let this guy look at me as if I'm some simpering fool. Even if I was acting like one.

Damien and Ryan had told me this agent has incredible skills and years of training, and I give him a slow, thorough once-over, taking in his wind-ruffled hair, faded jeans, and the long-sleeved scoop-neck shirt that hugs his pecs in a way that suggests he has some serious muscle.

He doesn't react to my inspection—which, honestly, impresses me. Most men are intimidated by me. It's a perk of the job.

"Dining room," he says. "You're holding up the show."

My brows rise. "It's my house."

"It's my time."

I cock my head, not sure if I'm annoyed or amused. But there is no way I'm losing this battle. "You were late getting here in the first place."

"I wasn't late," he says. The corner of his mouth twitches, and my always-fast temper ratchets up a notch. "I was walking the perimeter."

"On *my* time," I repeat.

He takes a step toward me, and I have to resist the urge to back away. Like most men, he's a few inches taller than me. Usually, that doesn't matter. Usually, I always feel like the tallest person in the room.

With Simon Barré, that isn't the case.

"The time is mine," he says, his voice low and steady. "At the end of the day, time is all any of us have."

I take a step back, surprised. I wasn't expecting those words. That thought. The same words, more or less, that I'd thrown at my manager when I turned down a piece-of-crap blockbuster that would have paid enough to buy my own island. No private island is worth those hours I would never get back.

I swallow, then speak despite my suddenly dry mouth. "It's my money that's paying for your time." Despite all my theatrical skills, the words do not come out with the intensity I'd intended.

He studies me, then nods slowly. "Very well. I guess I'm yours. Tell me what I'm supposed to do."

I draw myself up, my shoulders going back automatically. "Excuse me?" It's the tone that usually makes people scurry in fear. My secret weapon against an industry that treats me like property. Nothing more than an asset on the balance sheet. I learned a long time ago how to protect myself and control my destiny, and it's second nature to slide into the fortress I built around myself as a child. My safe place. And I always erect those walls to perfection.

Somehow, Simon Barré has toppled them, and instead of backing away with a muttered apology, he's coming closer. "You're scared, right?" To my surprise, I hear both sympathy and kindness in his voice. "I'm here because I was assigned to protect you. So that you'll be less scared." He pauses, waiting for me to acknowledge his words. Against my every instinct, I nod. "Well," he continues, the soft tone replaced by sharp edges, "tell me how to protect you. Tell me what the plan is."

"I don't know the plan," I snap.

"You don't?"

He slides his hands in the pockets of his jeans, and my eyes follow, noting the way the denim clings to his legs, his hips, his everything. I feel an unwelcome quickening of desire, and I snap my eyes back up to his.

"Are you saying I do?" he asks. "Know how to protect you, I mean."

My head is spinning. "Um, yes. That's why you're here. That's why I'm paying you."

Those green eyes flash with temper. And maybe a hint of victory. "Then get back to the dining table, stay there, and let me do my job. Because believe me when I say I never signed on to play babysitter to a diva."

That's it. "What the *hell* is your problem?"

"Right now, it's you. You're holding up our meeting."

The door swings open, and we both turn to see Aaron step in. "Did you two get lost?"

Aaron Kepler is ten years older than me, with pale blue eyes, a straggly beard, and an easy smile. Most important, he's been in my life for almost as long as I can remember. He was fresh out of college and working as a production assistant on *Bright Eyes* when I was ten and the show was just starting. He became like a brother to me and my bestie, Carolyn, the showrunner's daughter, who also had a recurring role as the next-door neighbor.

I close my eyes, gathering myself the way I always do when I think about Carolyn and that horrible night.

"Frannie?"

I look up, startled to find Aaron right in front of me, his expression full of concern. He might now be the president of Freeway Flix, a streaming service with its own production arm that is giving Netflix a run for its money, but he's still just Aaron to me.

I shake off my mood and meet his eyes, then watch as his attention moves from me to my jerk of a bodyguard, then back to me. He frowns as he searches my face, probably afraid I'm about to fly off the handle. He knows me well, after all.

But he also has a tendency toward overprotection, and I don't need him playing savior. Mr. Barré really isn't worth the trouble.

"We're doing fine. Since Simon here is going to be my bodyguard, we were getting to know each other."

"Yeah, well, I think they want you both back in there."

"Right," says the Captain America wannabe.

I sigh, then follow both men back into the dining area where command central is set up at my dining table, a huge, heavy thing that the designer I'd hired picked "because it suited my status" after I became a newly minted Academy Award winner. It's supposed to make me happy—a reminder of that awesome night. Instead, it just irritates me.

Damien and Ryan are there, along with my long-time friend Matthew Holt. A force of nature in the entertainment industry, Holt is a triple threat, and through his company, Hardline Entertainment, he has fingers in the music, film, and television industries. Plus, Hardline owns Freeway and is providing most of the financing for my next two films, both of which will have a short theatrical run before streaming exclusively at Freeway.

Matthew's brilliant, with a well-earned reputation for being dangerous. I've seen that famous temper more than once. And while I don't believe the rumor that he actually killed a man, it wouldn't surprise me to learn that it's true.

As a friend, Matthew's here to support me. As a businessman, he's here because I may be in danger, and since I'm slated to star in several Hardline films, that could be bad for business. Which is why he's covering some of the cost of making sure I stay alive.

They are the only three at the table, five when Aaron and Simon join them. There are other agents in the room, though, all gathered near the doorway as they study tablets or talk into headsets, presumably conferring with the indoor and outdoor agents and techies who are checking and upgrading my security.

Damien looks up, his forehead creased in a frown. He may have founded Stark Security, but I know he doesn't usually work the actual jobs, and I appreciate him being here. We're not close friends, but we've gotten to know each other over the years, and I respect him and his wife.

"Something wrong?" he asks.

I shake my head. "Other than the fact that some dickwad has

threatened my life? What could possibly be wrong?"

"Right now, you're safe," Ryan says. "Simon's going to stay here with you to make sure you stay that way."

"Oh, goody."

"The man's excellent at his job," Damien adds, his voice casual. As if he's just making conversation and not smoothing my ruffled feathers. Honestly, if he hadn't become some huge tech billionaire, he could have been a diplomat.

"No one can be that good." I shoot Simon a sour look that would have melted a lesser man. He just regards me mildly as I continue my rant, my temper—and my fear—rising. "This is not someone rational we're talking about. They're a loose cannon. Who knows what they'll do? A sniper rifle. A bomb in my car. Hell, a miniature nuclear weapon dropped on my—"

"Francesca. Calm down." It's Aaron, and his calm irritates the crap out of me. He's handling me. And I hate being handled.

"She's right—"

I whip around to face Simon, who's stood and is now pacing. "Don't you dare dismiss my—wait. What?"

He pauses, his brows rising. "I said you're right." He looks at Ryan, then Damien. "And she is. Hell, I told her the same thing when she was standing in front of a window." He crosses to where the matching buffet for my pretentious table sits against the wall. He hops up and sits on it, his heels lightly tapping on the polished teak.

"Do you mind?" I snap. More because his familiar attitude annoys me than because I give a flip about the buffet. That and the fact that even as much as I despise the table and buffet, I could never bring myself to sit on it like that. They're reminders of what I've accomplished. What I've gained.

And, most of all, the secrets I've put firmly behind me.

Or I thought I had. Until this morning when the note arrived.

"She's right about our perp," he says, ignoring me. "The note didn't say *Keep your mouth shut and stay alive*. It said *You tell, or you die*. He's starting from a place of danger. Or she. But odds are it's a man. And maybe that note means nothing. Maybe he was just trying to be dramatic and wouldn't hurt a fly. But he has an agenda, and he's making threats. We need to take him seriously."

"And we are," Ryan said. "That's why you're here."

"Exactly," Matthew continues, then turns to face Simon. "You're her bodyguard. Around the clock, right?"

"And not just him," I say. "There will be a whole team tomorrow, right? Because those cons get crowded, and—"

"Whoa, whoa," Matthew says, holding up his hands. "You are not going to the con. The crowds? Anything could happen."

"Of course I'm going. Some of these folks flew across the country to see me. They've paid extra to go to my panel, and then a surplus on top of that for the photo-op and autograph session."

I glance at Simon to see him looking at me, his brow furrowed. "What?" I snap.

But he doesn't answer, because Matthew jumps in first. "They'll survive. It's fandom. It's not the end of the world if they don't get their picture taken with you."

I shake my head. "No. Forget it. I am not disappointing them."

"So you're going to put yourself in danger?" Matthew snaps. "Come on, Frannie. You don't even like doing the Blue Zenith movies. You're the one who says the best thing about them is that they pay for the smaller films."

"Yes. Exactly." I turn to Damien and Ryan, wanting their help, but it's Simon who starts to speak. And since I know *exactly* what Mr. Rambo-Ass-Idiot is going to say, I whip back around to face Aaron and Matthew.

"That is *exactly* why it's important to go," I tell them. "Because even though I'm not a fan of superhero movies, we both know they pay the bills and keep the studio in business. Not because they exist in the world, but because fans go in droves. *These* fans. And that means it's these fans—not either of you—who are funding the movies I *am* passionate about. And that means I care about these fans. Deeply."

I think about *Spiraling*, my current passion project. A weird little Sci-Fi piece about a woman losing her mind as she watches her body slowly disappear. She does riskier and riskier things to try and keep her purchase on earth. It's funky and bizarre and beautifully written. The next Blue Zenith movie might pay the bills. But *Spiraling* speaks to me. And I'll be damned if I'll let some bastard with a poison pen keep me from working.

I look at each of them in turn, then pull Damien, Ryan, and Simon in under the force of my glare. "You all need to listen to me and understand. There is no way—*zero way*—I am going to let those fans down. They are my bread and butter, and I'm going to be there for them. You can't stop me, but if you're really concerned, you can damn well protect me. That's what this meeting's about, right?"

"Dammit, Frannie," Matthew says, "you can't play fast and loose with your well-being. You're worth too much, and insurance won't—"

"Oh, thank you for your concern," I snap. "I thought we were talking as friends, but nice to know all I am to you is an ATM."

To his credit, Matthew looks like he wants to eat his own tongue.

"You know that's not what he meant," Aaron said. "But he's right that insurance won't cover—"

"Insurance has no idea that we're aware of a threat." I look between all the men, daring them to challenge me again. "I am going to that con. You can have security hanging from the ceiling if you want to, but I will be there."

Matthew stares daggers at me. "Those things are crowded and crazy and—"

"And important to my fans."

"They'll survive." His voice is hard and firm. "Don't you think they'd rather you be alive than—"

"They want to meet me. They paid money to meet me, and—"

"She's right."

I whip around to gape at Simon. "Damn right, I am," I say. "But, um, I'm surprised you're agreeing with me."

He meets my eyes. Holds them. One second, then another.

I look away. *What the hell is wrong with me? I never look away.*

Ryan clears his throat. "Honestly, I'm surprised, too. Simon, explain."

Simon glances once more at me, but this time I don't meet his gaze. Then he reaches for the piece of paper I received that morning. A pale brown sheet with thick lines that looks like it was ripped from the kind of Big Chief notebook that little kids use. *"You tell, or you die."* He reads the words scrawled in awkward handwriting, presumably from someone using their non-dominant hand.

"Thank you, but I can read," I snap.

"Dammit, Ms. Muratti. Someone's threatening to kill you." His tone brings me up short. For a moment, I think he might actually care if that happens. Then again, I suppose my death would be a professional disappointment.

I flash him my most dangerous glare. "Do you think I don't know that? Do you think I'm not scared? Of course, I am. But I meant what I said. Those fans deserve to see me. Some of them have traveled from other countries, and I'm not letting them down. I thought you were on my—"

"I'm not asking you to let them down. And if you'd quit being enchanted by the sound of your own voice—"

"What the hell?"

"And *listen*, you would know that I am not suggesting you stay away. It's fine for you to attend the con. With me as your escort, of course. And a team in the background, just in case."

"Are you crazy?" Matthew asks, at the same time that Aaron says, "Whoa—wait just a damn minute."

"I can go?" I'm totally revising my opinion of this guy.

"Simon," Ryan says, his voice mild. But there's an edge to it.

"No," Simon snaps back. "You assigned me this case. I'm running it my way, or you assign someone else."

I see a muscle twitch in Ryan's cheek. "Then tell us what you're thinking."

"It's tomorrow. This event she's going to is tomorrow." He spreads his hand and shrugs as he looks at everyone, as if that explains everything.

It doesn't, but since I have no intention of saying anything to turn Simon off of the Let's Go To Con plan, I say nothing. Damien Stark, however, isn't so trusting. He leans back in his chair, cocks his head, and says, "Explain."

Simon exhales loudly, and right then, I know that he thinks he's the smartest person in the room. Which, if he convinces the others he's right, I'll be prepared to agree with. Damien, however, isn't used to being behind the curve, and I can see the curiosity—and the frustration—on that gorgeous face.

"The damn letter came today. *Today*. Now maybe the sender is just a one hundred percent whack job, but let's assume there's a shred of rationality. If so, he's not going to make his move just yet."

Ryan nods slowly. "He'll give Frannie time to not only decide what to do, but also to figure out what it is she's supposed to tell. You're certain you don't know?"

"You've all asked me that a hundred times," I say. "I told you. No idea. I mean, yeah, I know some scandalous shit—you can't work in this industry at the level I do and not hear stuff—but nothing I can imagine anyone would kill for."

"Whoever sent that note must know that. He—or she," Simon added, "will have factored that in. He'll give you time to think before he gets dangerous. I'd bet my reputation on it."

"And my life?" I ask. "Are you willing to bet my life?"

Simon has been looking at Ryan, but now he turns back to me. Whatever friction was between us in the kitchen, it's gone now. The man is pure professional. "I am. But only because it's a bet I don't expect to lose. I already told you about the timing, but that doesn't mean we won't have precautions. Like not walking into your kitchen when the security system is down."

I cross my arms and glare, but I get the point.

"And as for the con, there will be metal detectors at the door and a full team of undercover and uniformed security. I checked."

"Really?" Despite myself, I'm impressed. I didn't realize he knew about the con, much less that he'd researched it.

"So I guess the question is for you," Simon says. "Are *you* willing to bet your life on my judgment?"

I draw in a breath, letting his words roll over me. I could issue an apology. I could disappoint all those fans. But the thing is, I think this Simon must be right. No one's going to come after me this soon. Because I really *don't* know what the threat refers to. *You tell, or you die.* But tell what? And who's going to do the killing?

I only hope I can figure that out soon enough.

"Well?" Aaron says, his voice like a gunshot in the silent room.

"Yeah," I say, looking only at Simon, and hoping like hell he can really help me. "Yeah, I'll take that bet."

Chapter Two

He didn't want to like her.

He really, really, *really* didn't want to like her.

She was a self-involved, conceited, money-hungry star who lived in a fantasy world and didn't know a damn thing about real people or real problems. Just like every other actor in this fucked-up town.

He knew it. Was certain of it. He was familiar with the type, after all. Hadn't they destroyed his childhood? Ripped away his fiancée?

Oh, yeah. He knew better than to like or trust this breed, and Francesca Muratti was no exception. She was just one more spoiled actress who'd caught the eye of a nut job with a grudge against spoiled actresses.

And yet...

He bit back a grimace, hating that he had to acknowledge those two little words. *And yet...*

And yet this spoiled, insufferable star was willing to put her life on the line to keep her fans happy.

This self-involved woman who made a living play-acting actually understood that the only reason she could enjoy the privilege of the life she had built was because she'd been lifted onto her pedestal by those fans. More than that, she not only understood it, but she was willing to risk literally everything to offer her thanks to those fans the only way she knew how—by being there for them.

He didn't have to like her. Hell, he *didn't* like her.

But he damn well respected her.

"All right," he said, hopping down from the buffet and moving to stand opposite her across the table. "We've settled that you're going to the con." He glanced around the room, making sure no one intended to keep up the argument. When all remained silent, he nodded. "Good. That means we're to the final point on today's agenda." He met Francesca's eyes. "Who sent the note? And what does he want you to reveal?"

He kept his attention locked on her, so there was no missing either the way her eyes widened just a hair or the slash of fury that cut across her undeniably beautiful face.

"Do I need to write you a song?" she snapped. "Do a tap dance? Or maybe you want me to tattoo the answer on my forehead. Some asshat wants me to say some magic words or else he's going to kill me, and I. Do. Not. Know. What. They. Are."

A tear snaked down her cheek, and she swiped it away, the gesture both angry and impatient.

"I can't tell what I don't know." She spoke directly to him, and he took the challenge, moving closer until he was breathing her air and could smell the lilac in her perfume.

"That's kind of my point, sweetheart," he said, studying her expression. Every tiny tick, every movement of her eyes. "I think you do."

"Excuse me?" She glared at him. The kind of look designed to melt a lesser man.

Too bad for her, he wasn't a lesser man. "You heard me," he repeated.

Sparks flew from her eyes. Not literally, but he could damn sure imagine them. He said nothing. Just looked back at her mildly, keeping his own temper in check. He was an expert at not showing his feelings, and that was a skill that would come in handy with Francesca Muratti. Probably more than his dead-on aim with a pistol.

With a huff, she turned to face Ryan, then Damien. "Assign another agent, or I'm firing the lot of you."

"And here I thought you liked me. What with convincing them to let you go to the con."

She whirled on him. "You insufferable prick. Don't you dare—"

"Frannie. Calm down." Damien's voice was low. Reasonable. And Simon was absolutely positive that was the wrong approach to take.

"Are you fucking kidding me, Stark? The man just called me a liar to my face. I have no idea—*zero theories*—as to what's going on, and he's accusing me of...well, fuck him. Fuck all of you. *Dammit.*"

She blinked, her lips pressed tight together as she spun away, giving all of them her back. And for a moment—a very, very fleeting moment— Simon had the urge to put his hands on her shoulders and tell her that it would all work out.

"Frannie," Damien said softly, "we're going to get to the bottom of this."

Her shoulders shook, and as much as she grated on him, he also knew that she was truly afraid. And because he was a damned idiot, his heart softened a little. At least until she spoke again.

"I don't want him here." The words were low. Barely audible. "He's an arrogant prick, and I don't want him in my home. For that matter," she added, turning to look at Damien and Ryan in turn, "I don't want anyone here. I got some stupid note, and I freaked, okay? But I shouldn't have, because there's nothing for me to tell. *Nothing.* Which means it's a prank. A joke. I'm safe. So go. All of you." She shifted, eyeing everyone in the room. "Go on," she snapped, her voice rising. "Get out of my house."

Nobody moved.

"*Dammit, go.*" A stray tear snaked down her cheek. Damian started to stand, but Simon stepped forward, cutting his boss off. He'd triggered this with his typically brash bullshit. Yeah, dealing with Hollywood types was as much fun as dragging his fingernails down a chalkboard, but there was no denying the woman was legitimately scared.

"Oh, come *on,*" she said as he approached her. "Won't you please just go?"

He pulled a chair out for her, then gestured for her to sit, surprised when she actually complied. He squatted down, one hand holding the table for balance, so that she didn't have to look up at him. Across the table, in his peripheral vision, he saw Stark and Ryan exchange a glance. Matthew Holt and Aaron were as still as stone. He remembered that Francesca was rumored to have a fiery temper on set; presumably, they were preparing for the explosion. As for the rest of the team, they'd long ago slipped out of the room. Good.

"Hear me out," Simon said, his attention now entirely on her. "Then, if you still want us to leave, we will."

He paused, giving her time to answer, and was relieved by her small nod of consent.

"You say you don't know what the note is referring to and that it must be a bad joke. A prank."

"That's the only thing that makes sense," she whispered, so low he had to strain to hear her.

"And you may be right. But the flip side is that you're wrong." He lifted a hand, halting her before she spoke. "Just hear me out. If you don't know what the note is referring to, that makes it *more* dangerous, not less.

Presume it's legit. By not answering—by doing nothing—you're basically flipping the guy off. And an angry stalker is a dangerous stalker."

"That's all conjecture. It's bullshit. Why am I the only one who sees that?"

Simon drew a breath. She was fighting back and pissing him off, and as much as he wanted to tell himself it was because she was a spoiled little Hollywood starlet, that wasn't the case. It was because she'd been threatened, and she was scared.

"I get that you wish all this would go away. I get that you're scared. But even if you really don't know what this thing is you're supposed to know, someone thinks you do. You're not safe. You can't control the scenario, and you need help. If you don't want me, that's fine. You take that up with these nice gentlemen here. I promise you I don't like the situation any more than you do."

"Barré." That from Ryan.

"He's signaling that I'm being unprofessional, and maybe he's right. But right now, I'm not interested in doing my job. I'm interested in making sure you feel comfortable and safe in your own house and at tomorrow's event. That means you need someone here for the safe part, and you need someone you trust for the comfortable part. Right now, both those roles are mine. But you say the word, and they'll find someone else."

He turned to look at the two men who'd recruited him. Who signed his extremely nice paycheck. Who'd told him he was assigned to this job even though he'd rather eat glass than work with an actress, much less the biggest actress on screen today. And he wondered just how much he'd pissed them off.

Maybe in the end, it didn't matter. Neither he nor Francesca wanted him here. She said the word, and he was history.

He drew a breath. "That's it. That's my speech. There's evidence that you're in danger, and you say you don't know why. All the more reason for someone to be with you."

"You said I'll be safe tomorrow."

"And I believe that. But I might be wrong. More important, I'm not just talking about tomorrow. I'm talking about the day after, and the day after that. All the way until we figure out who's harassing you. And right now, all those days—and all those nights—are on me. If you want someone else, now's the time to say so."

"Then I want Leah," she said, and he was shocked by the disappointment that slammed against him. "Have Leah move in."

Simon pulled out another chair and sat opposite her, then turned his attention to Ryan. She'd really rather have Leah than him? Leah was a solid agent, no doubt. But she was a small woman. Hardly the forbidding presence that could deter a hostile attack.

Still, if he was off the case, that would be a good thing. And this Hollywood princess would no longer be his problem.

"It makes sense," she continued, making her case to Ryan and Damien. "I know you think having a guy is better, but I know her socially. We can say she's staying at my place because she's remodeling. That she's shadowing me because she's writing a screenplay. Anything."

Ryan glanced at Damien and shrugged.

"I'm not sure I like that idea," Holt said. "I'm sure Leah is excellent at her job—and don't lay into me about being sexist—but Simon's a big man, and if Frannie's going to have a bodyguard..."

"Leah can handle herself," Ryan said. "We were playing the boyfriend card, but the best friend ploy works, too."

They all looked to Aaron, as if he had the final say, and Simon wondered about his relationship with Francesca. Just business, or did those two have a history?

He winced, realizing the direction of his thoughts. Why the hell did he care if they slept together?

"All right, Barré," Ryan said, the words getting Simon's thoughts back where they should be. "You're off the case. We'll get Leah, and—"

"*No.*" It took a moment for Simon to realize he was the one who'd uttered that one strong syllable. "No," he repeated, not quite able to believe what he was saying. Clearly Francesca couldn't believe it, either, if the way she was gaping at him was any indication.

"But you just said—"

"I know," he told her. "But Matthew's right. It's better to have a guy with you. It's better to have *me* with you," he added, not sure if he was saying it because the words were true or because he resented that look of pure relief he'd seen on her face when Ryan had agreed about Leah. "The assignment is mine."

Francesca's eyes were wide. "Then why did you suggest—"

"I'm sorry. I changed my mind. The boyfriend ploy is better. And, honestly, there's no one you should trust more than me to keep you safe."

Her brows rose. "I'm betting Damien and Ryan disagree with you about that. Not to mention all the other agents at Stark Security."

He shrugged. "Probably, but this is the way it's going to be." He turned to face Ryan and Damien. "Maybe it's just a hoax and there's no real danger, but if there is, then Ms. Muratti wants me."

"No, I—"

"Yes," he insisted, turning his attention back to her. "I've got my issues with Hollywood, but they aren't personal. I'm sorry if I've been an ass," he said sincerely. "I'm usually more professional, and I will be going forward. Because you need to keep me on," he continued, his mouth continuing to blather on even while all of his common sense told him to take the opening and run, run, run away from this Hollywood ice queen.

Apparently, his listening skills were for shit, because he didn't run. Instead, he just kept talking. "And, sure, Leah's got skills. But I've been doing this longer, and I'm a better option. I've done this before. Protected celebrities and power players from threats from unknown sources. Plus a lot of other jobs I can't tell you about, but that I promise will help me to keep you safe."

He paused to study her face, satisfied when he saw that she was listening. Really listening. As for Damien and Ryan, hopefully he'd still have a job when he shut up because otherwise, he'd be working freelance. Damn him for letting his personal feelings get in the way of client safety.

He knew better. It was this Hollywood bullshit. That whole goddamn business. But he was bigger than the industry. Bigger than his past. And he was determined to protect this woman.

"Mr. Barré," she began, but he cut her off.

"No. Let me finish. If this somehow went south and I wasn't on it, I'd never forgive myself. And neither would you, because you'd be dead. This threat is bigger than we first realized, and I'm staying on it," he said firmly and was surprised to see respect in Francesca's eyes where he'd expected irritation. "I'm the man for this job. And I'm not taking no for an answer."

"Frannie?" Ryan asked from behind him.

"Yes," she said. "He'll do." She drew in a breath and sat up straighter, her shoulders going back in a way that made her look both regal and powerful. "But why do you say the threat's bigger?" She looked at him, then glanced over his shoulder at Ryan and Damien, neither of whom answered her question.

"Because you know something," he told her. Then hurried on when she opened her mouth to respond. "I'm not saying you can pull it out of the sky right now, but you do know something. You saw something or overheard something—or you were in a position to. However it went down, someone is convinced that you have knowledge. Something they want to know as well, and they want it enough to threaten you."

"But I don't know wha—"

"I believe you. But here's the thing. Someone is threatening to kill you if you *don't* tell. That also means there must be someone who wants that secret held close. Someone your antagonist is trying to intimidate or blackmail or ruin. And once that person learns that their secret may come out—"

"I'll have someone who wants me to stay silent just as much as our Mr. X wants me to talk."

"Bingo," he said, flashing her a smile. Not because of the danger, but because right then—for just a few heartbeats—they were actually working together. "There are two threats against you, even if one isn't viable yet. Two very serious threats."

"He's right," Ryan said as Damien nodded in silent agreement.

"Yes," Francesca said. "I'm afraid he is."

"That's why I'm not walking away. It's why you're stuck with me and not Leah. But we will find out who's behind this," he said. "I promise."

"I'm all for that," Francesca said. "But I don't see how."

"That's where the fun part comes in," he said with a smirk. "You and I will be getting to know each other pretty well over the next few days. Because we're going to dig into your life. We're going to dig deep. And we're going to figure out what it is that somebody thinks you know."

Chapter Three

"Try not to kill each other," Ryan says as we linger in the entryway by my front door. Matthew and Aaron left over an hour ago, and Damien left after kissing me lightly on the cheek and telling me not to worry. I said I'd try, but I'm making no promises.

"Just make sure you remember what an excellent client I am. And how much I'm willing to put up with," I add, glancing over my shoulder toward Simon, who's on the other side of the room leaning against the archway that separates the entry from the casual living area. "Think about that when you send my next bill."

He chuckles. "I'll keep it in mind. Seriously, though, I've already told Simon I expect daily reports, and I want to hear from you, as well, and not just to bitch."

I raise a brow. "But I have so much to complain about."

"He's good, Frannie."

"I believe you. I was joking."

"I get that you two may rub each other the wrong way personally, but he's on this assignment because both Damien and I trust that he can keep you safe. And he's right. He's the best choice for the job. Promise."

I smile. The one that flashes with real emotion. Not the one I've practiced for photo ops. "I know. I agreed, right? And seriously, thanks. Tell Jamie congrats for me. She's really taking off."

Pride shines in his eyes as his own smile lights his face. "She really is. She was starting to believe she'd never land a starring role in a major movie, and now it's about to start shooting."

"But you never doubted."

"No," he agrees. "I never did. I have good instincts that way." He puts a hand on my shoulder. "Simon has good instincts, too. I want your word you'll trust him."

"I'm paying for those instincts, aren't I? Of course, I'll trust them."

"Frannie…"

"Yes," I say, without the crassness of cash mucking up my words. "I will let the man do his job and keep me alive. But if he fails, I'm coming back to haunt all of you."

His cheek dimples with his smile. "I'll keep that in mind. And Frannie, for God's sake, if you think of something that might help, just tell him. Don't overthink it. If he changes his mind and tells you that you need to leave the con tomorrow, you do it. Remember, we'll have a team there, backing him up. You're covered, okay?"

"You're just chattering to run up my hourly bill," I tease, giving him a quick hug. "Now go."

This time, he really does, and when I turn around after closing the door behind him, Simon is nowhere to be seen. Great. The moment I'm alone, my bodyguard disappears.

I frown, fully intending to give Simon grief for disappearing after fighting so hard to be the point guy. But then he steps through the arch and walks toward me, looking for all the world like he owns the damn room.

"Where were you five seconds ago?"

"You were talking with Ryan. I made myself scarce. I thought you might need a final moment to complain about me," he adds, the corner of his lip twitching.

"You thought right," I say, fighting my own laughter. I hesitate, then clear my throat. "Listen, I get that we rub each other the wrong way. I'm not sure if it's our personalities or the situation, but it's the truth. Even so, there is one thing we agree on—we don't want me dead. Me for obvious reasons, and you because I'm sure you'd get ribbed at work if I end up a corpse."

"Yes, the hazing would be unbearable. That's definitely my primary motivation."

I ignore him. "So let's just latch on to our mutual desire to keep me breathing and go from there."

He's standing beside the round table that dominates the middle of the entryway, and he takes four long steps toward me, which puts him close enough that I can practically hear his heartbeat, and the proximity is disconcerting.

I don't, however, move. That would be giving in, and that's

something I never do. At least not unless there's an advantage to me.

"Mutual desire," he says, his voice pitched low. Sensual.

"Excuse me?" My head is spinning, and I've forgotten what we were talking about.

"You said we shared a mutual desire." He moves even closer. "A desire to keep you alive. And we do. So you listen to me, Francesca. You do what I say. You obey my instructions. You answer my questions so we can find whoever is sending you those letters. You do that for me, and we'll both get what we want."

And then, while I'm standing in my entryway blinking like a fool, my mouth completely dry, he turns and walks into the great room, his words flowing back to me. "We're leaving in ten. If you want to change, now's the time to do it."

"Leaving?" For a moment, I simply gape, then I hurry after him, my heels clicking on the tile. "There's an entire team outside upgrading my home into a fortress, and we're just going to leave?"

"One, the job is to keep you safe, not hold you prisoner." He tilts his head as if studying me. "I believe you made that point yourself not half an hour ago with the con. You pretty much threatened a mutiny if anyone tries to hold you back."

I grimace because he's right.

Even so, I aim my most domineering glare at him now. "I have a specific reason for going to the con. As far as I know, your outing is nothing more than a jaunt for you to go grab a donut."

"I need to run by my place."

"Excuse me?"

He slides his hands into the pockets of his jeans and leans casually against my wall. "I need my things."

I blink as I realize the bigger ramifications of his words. "Wait. You're staying here?"

One brow rises, giving him a decidedly rakish appearance. "You expected me to stick close and protect you from the nearest Motel 6?"

The truth is, I hadn't thought about it at all except in some vague way. Like taking my morning walk on the beach with him behind me in a leather coat and dark glasses, fresh out of Central Casting.

Or better, maybe I'll be out to dinner, and he'll be standing casually behind me in a suit. I can get on board with that. Because no matter what else he might be, Simon Barré is the kind of man every designer imagines. A guy who projects a rugged elegance. The kind of man who could make any outfit look good.

I clear my throat, realizing that my thoughts have gone dangerously and uncomfortably astray. "So go. I can stay here. The property is crawling with agents right now. They're still doing all that outside stuff, right?"

"No," he says.

"They're not?"

"You're not staying." His eyes are on mine, and I expect him to elaborate. He doesn't; instead, he simply holds my gaze. Not a challenge so much as an exploration.

I match him, but it's not easy, which surprises me. I'm the woman who stares down anyone who dares to gawk at me. I genuinely love my fans, but I don't love feeling like a bug under glass. Still, I know it's an inherent part of celebrity—that sense of being on display, that other people feel entitled to look you up and down as if they're judging the size of your ass and the knobbiness of your knees. Sometimes, it's just a fan, basking in being *that close* to someone they've let into their homes so often the actor truly feels like an old friend.

But most of the time, the glances feel assessing—as if they're determined to find a flaw. As if the fact that I might have a blemish makes them a better person. Or it feels pervy, like all I've been doing my whole career is providing a mental picture for some dude to jack off to.

That's not how it feels with Simon.

His gaze feels appraising, yes, but also warm. Like he's seeing me for the first time. Not the me on screen but the real me I hide behind my eyes. And for a moment—one sweet, wonderful moment—I want to open to him. To share all my secrets and fears.

But that's me living one of the fantasies I play out on the screen. The kind where the hard and broken girl finally opens herself to the guy and finds true love.

That's not real life, though. That's just the movies.

I know that better than anyone.

This isn't the third act. He's not the hero. And the only reason he's looking at me with such intensity is because I'm a client and he's taking my measure.

I break first. "Just go. I'll be here when you get back, trapped in my house."

"You're coming with me."

"Why?"

He moves closer, and I have to fight the urge to back away and regain some of my personal space. "Because you're my responsibility," he says. His voice is gentle, but his eyes are hard. They've captured me, and I feel myself tumbling into their deep, green depths. And that, I think, is a dangerous kind of fall.

"Can we just fucking go?" I snap as I lurch backward, needing space between us. "Or is staring at me part of your master plan to keep me safe?"

"Sure. We can go," he says, stepping past me toward the door as if my words have no sting at all. "As for staring, I was just sussing you up."

"And?" The word's out of my mouth before I can think better of it.

"Eh," he says, then heads through the door, leaving me to follow as I nurse the unexpected sting left by that single, throwaway word.

Chapter Four

She was getting under his skin.

No doubt about that, and the simple truth annoyed the hell out of him. Francesca Muratti was gorgeous and snarky and irritating and fascinating, and he really didn't want to like her because he knew only too well whatever bits he actually did like were as fake as the chimera she projected onto screens all over the country.

So no, he didn't like her. But maybe he respected her. A little, anyway.

"Grab your purse if you need it," he said, pausing before opening the front door. "We'll go check in with the team, then head to my place."

"I'm not allowed to stand by myself in my own kitchen, but we're going to traipse around the yard instead of heading straight for your car?"

"Yeah, well, I'm over this assignment. Figured that was a good way to wrap up this gig fast."

She cocked her head and gave him a death stare, but he saw amusement in her eyes and, dammit, his respect for her ratcheted up a notch.

She grabbed a bag from a small table by the door and slung it over her arm. "Fine."

He waited for her to argue, and when she didn't, he opened the front door, then waited some more. Still no argument. Instead, she lifted her chin then stepped past him onto her massive front porch. He followed, more impressed by her courage than he wanted to admit. He was confident all was fine, but he could understand how she might still be nervous. And yet she was trusting him.

Or, if not trust, she was trying to prove something to him. Well, he'd take it.

"This way," he said, leading her down the steps, then along the path that led to the side yard. The fence had a code, and he entered it, then held the gate open as she stepped through. The fence was solid, surrounding three sides of her five-acre yard, with the fourth being a cliff drop-off to the beach below, which used to be accessible by an iron staircase. The team had removed it early that morning, and after the threat was neutralized, they'd re-install it. But in the interim, no one was sneaking up the cliff to Francesca's land.

As for the fence itself, it had provided a modicum of protection, but with the upgrades the team had finalized today, it was now state of the art.

They moved past the pool, her heels clicking on the tile decking. When he stepped off the tile and into the grass, he heard her sigh. "If you'd told me we were coming back here, we could have gone out the back door. Plus, I would have slipped on some loafers."

He turned to face her and watched as she kicked off the pale pink shoes, then left them on the deck as she moved quickly toward him, bare feet in the cut grass.

"You're not picking them up?"

She quirked a single, perfectly plucked brow. "You think they're going to get lonely?"

"Aren't they Jimmy Choos or something? Those things probably cost more than my car."

"They're Gucci, yes, but they're still shoes. I'm sure they'll survive the trauma of temporary abandonment. Well?" she said a moment later as he stood staring at her, stopped short by his surprise at her words. "What are we waiting for?"

A good question, and since his only answer was that he'd been waiting for the shock of liking her to fade, he ignored her and started to cross the yard, trusting her to keep up with him. Right now, she was a client. A potential victim. Of course he had empathy and professional concern. It would be later, when she put on the Hollywood hat, that his skin would prickle. It would happen. It was inevitable. And then it would be on him to stay professional. Because he wouldn't like *that* Francesca. He knew how selfish Hollywood types were. How willing they were to walk over anyone in order to get what they wanted. To lie. To cheat. To abandon the people they professed to love for nothing more than the promise of those lights and cameras.

Yeah, he knew the type well. So he'd protect Francesca because that was the job. But he damn sure wouldn't like her.

He glanced down, not wanting her to see his expression, then noticed that without the shoes, the hem of those perfectly tailored silk slacks was dragging in the grass, and she didn't even seem to care. He felt his whole body tighten, not certain if he was disgusted by her casual treatment of something so expensive, or impressed that she clearly wasn't one of those women whose entire day might be ruined by a grass stain.

He remembered when Kristen got the job at the agency, then came home insisting that she had to revamp her entire wardrobe because she had to look like someone who should be in front of the camera, not behind a desk. He'd been amused at first, assuming she was joking, but after that—

"Simon?"

"What?" he snapped, feeling a tinge of guilt that he was taking his personal shit out on her. But she was a Hollywood ice queen. She could take it. Thick skins, massive egos, and a hell of a survival instinct. The defining characteristics of those who thrived in LaLa Land. He'd seen it firsthand, after all.

She hesitated, looking around the yard. He saw Mario and the rest of the team by the cliff's drop-off and assumed she'd head that direction. Instead, she hugged herself, then said, "You're really sure this is okay?"

Her voice was low, as if she was afraid the question would offend him. "I mean, I know Damien and Ryan trust you, and—Oh, hell. Are you really sure? That the outside is safe? For now at least?" Her voice rose in pitch so that there was no mistaking her genuine fear. "I mean, hey, I know you don't want this job, but your plan to trot me out for the slaughter seems a little much."

She managed a smile to show it was a joke, but there was no disguising the genuine worry in her voice. Honestly, she might as well have just punched him in the gut.

Without thinking, he took her hand, a bit surprised when she didn't pull away. Even more surprised when her fingers curled around his. "I'm sorry," he said, feeling like a complete prick. "I'm an ass, okay? As tempting as it might be to take the easy way off this case and toss you over that cliff, I promise you, it's safe. I should have told you so before we even stepped outside the house."

"But earlier you said the system was down, and—"

"Mario texted me. The system's back up and better than ever."

"*Should* have told me," she repeated. "Then why didn't you? You dislike me so much that you want me scared?"

"Honestly, it slipped my mind. But that's not even the point. You need to understand it's not a question of like or dislike. It's a question of you trusting me so that I can keep you safe. You don't get to second-guess my decisions or ask for my reasoning. If I say jump, you should feel safe to jump. If I say we're going outside, you say, *Yes, sir.* You don't have to worry about asking why or if it's safe." He drew a breath, fighting down the unwelcome image of Francesca naked on her knees, her lips curled around those words. *Yes, sir.*

He cleared his throat, banishing the unwelcome and very unlikely image. "We both have a job here," he said. "Mine is to assess and act and keep you safe. Yours is to trust me."

"Trust you?" Her mouth twisted into an ironic smile. "You don't even like me."

"Don't I?"

She lifted a brow and crossed her arms over her chest as if she was waiting for him to kiss the boo-boo and make it all better. Which meant she still didn't get it. "Like has nothing to do with it," he said. "Like doesn't factor in at all. I don't have to like you or the industry you work in to do my job. For that matter, you don't have to like me. But you do have to trust me, and you do have to obey."

"I'm not good at blindly following orders."

"Then you're a fool. You hired me for my skill and experience. I say jump, the only question you should ask is how high."

Her teeth grazed her lower lip.

"I mean it, Francesca. I'm good at what I do. You didn't hire me for my looks."

"Definitely not your looks," she said, her eyes raking over him in a way that seemed all too familiar and just a tad too appealing. "I mean, if we're talking first impressions, it's a miracle Ryan and Damien hired you at all."

"Excuse me?"

"That body? That face? Not to mention your hair and your oh-so perfect beard stubble." She threw off a shrug. "Bottom line, you're too damn pretty. You're made for a tumble in bed, not the cold, hard streets fighting bad guys."

The thought of a tumble in bed messed with his head way more than it should, and it took him a full five seconds before he could think clearly enough to shake his head slowly. "I'm entirely unsure if I should be flattered or insulted."

She shrugged. "Either works for me." She narrowed her eyes. "Although maybe you really are trying to get me killed. I get blown away, you move on to the next thing."

He took a step toward her. "Are you still worried? Because right now, I'm not. But I don't want to make you uncom—"

"No." She shook her head. "No. I'm just messing with you. Is it what you said before? About it being too soon? I mean, if you brought me out here, I know I'm safe. But what I want to know is why."

He felt an odd surge of pride. Coming from her, the question was a compliment. "A few things. First of all, like you said. It's too soon. But I don't want to rest entirely on that assessment, as sure as I might be."

"So there's more?"

"There's more." He pointed toward Mario and Jasper and the others, all of whom wore black T-shirts with *Stark Security* stenciled on the back in large white letters and the company logo on the front. "For one, the system is back on line like I told you, and those guys know what they're doing. Plus, there are notices surrounding the property in ten-foot increments that tell anyone who might be thinking about attacking that both your home and your property are protected."

He pointed to a few of the cameras mounted on trees, poles, and under the eaves of the house. "There are also outfacing cameras all along the perimeter, as well as a perimeter breach warning system. I'll grant you there's still the possibility of a breach by a long-range sniper, but I already told you why I think that's a minimal risk at the moment."

She grimaced. "This whole thing is probably some tabloid reporter's new scheme for getting all the dirt."

"It fits," he said. "Hollywood—destroying journalism one crappy headline at a time."

She rolled her eyes, then caught up as he started walking toward the cliff and the rest of the Stark Security team. "You think you're insulting me," she said, "but I agree with you. Entertainment reporting is a far cry from journalism. As for actors and current events, we tend to be a well-informed group."

"Glad to hear it. But we're not debating current events."

"Thank God for that."

He glanced over and saw her quick smile. At almost three, the sun was above them at an angle, and its rays brought out the auburn highlights in her velvet black hair. It hung loose around her face, softening her sculpted features. She was, in a word, beautiful. And it irritated the hell out of him that he not only noticed that, but was taking the time to think about it.

"—than a newspaper."

He shook himself out of his trance. "Sorry. What?"

She shot him an exasperated glance. "How you're going to protect me if you can't even pay attention to me is entirely beyond my ability to comprehend."

"That doesn't surprise me."

She wrinkled the perfect nose that probably cost a fortune. "I was saying that even though I stay up on the news, on the whole, I'd rather read a book than a newspaper."

"Yeah? I would have thought you'd say a screenplay."

She gave a little shudder. "Hardly. That's for work. Books are leisure."

"Bet you read lots of adaptations." He kept a straight face, knowing he was baiting her.

"No."

He came to a stop, taking her hand and pulling her to a halt beside him. For a moment, he thought she was going to stay like that, her hand in his, soft and warm. Then she glanced down, raised her brows, and tugged her hand free.

Across the lawn, Mario looked toward them, his hand raised in a silent question. Simon ignored him; what else could he do? He was busy baiting the movie star, and, honestly, having a hell of a lot more fun with her than he'd expected. "All right, princess," he said. "Tell me what you're reading right now."

"*The Stand.* Stephen King."

"Of course you are. The most adapted man on the planet." He had no idea if that was true, but it seemed like a reasonable guess.

"The books came first. I got addicted to him when I was a kid. Read *Carrie*, got hooked, and I've been reading and re-reading him ever since."

"So you're into horror. What else?"

"Psychological thrillers. *Gone Girl* was great."

"Another adaptation."

She wrinkled her nose but otherwise ignored him.

"And I read romance. I'm reading a fabulous Regency series by Darcy Burke. The Untouchables."

"So it's another adaptation. Brian DePalma, Costner, De Niro, Connery. Come on, Francesca, just admit it. With you, it's all about the flicks."

"Wrong story. I told you. It's a Regency romance series, and it's awesome."

"But not adapted?"

"No," she said, "but it should be."

"There you go. A typical Hollywood gal. All about the adaption."

"No, dammit, you're not hearing me. I'm—"

He couldn't help the laugh that escaped.

Her eyes widened. "I *will* get you back."

"You can try," he said, then hurried across the lawn toward Mario while she tried to keep up with his long strides.

And the weirdest thing of all? He couldn't remember the last time he'd had so much fun teasing a woman.

Chapter Five

"I couldn't understand half of what Mario was saying," I tell Simon as he maneuvers the flat streets of North Hollywood in a ridiculously boring Honda hybrid. Honestly, if I'd had to guess, I would have picked Simon for having the typical jerky male penis-mobile. So I'm not entirely sure if I'm impressed that he's not all about the flash or disappointed that I read him wrong.

We've been out of the Malibu hills for a while, and I'm still reeling a bit with how light and easy our conversation has been for the past hour. We've talked about everything from my mysterious tormentor to local restaurants to my utterly failed attempt at surfing. Weirdly, he's easy to talk to, something I didn't expect after our initial prickly encounters.

Then again, he's probably doing the same thing I am—sucking it up for the sake of the job. After all, we're stuck together. Might as well make the best of it.

"I'm pretty sure English is his second language," Simon says, pulling me back to my comment about Mario. "He was born speaking geek. And he speaks it damn well."

"It sounded impressive, that's for sure." I think about the dark-haired man with the easy smile and intelligent eyes. "He's so young, though. He heads up the entire Stark Security tech team?"

"He looks young, but I think he's in his early thirties, and yeah. On the tech side, he's the guy in charge. Pretty sure he started out as one of Stark's protégés at Stark Applied Technology, then moved over here. The guy knows his stuff."

"Hmm." I glance at Simon, trying to judge his age.

"What?"

"Nothing."

"Bullshit," he said. "You're wondering about my resume."

"I am not," I lie. "Except, okay, yeah. I am. I mean, I trust Damien and Ryan, but…well, I have no idea why you're qualified to do this," I say, gesturing at myself.

That dimple of his appears. "This being you?" We're at a red light, and he turns his head to look at me, his eyes skimming lightly over me, all the way from my head to my toes. "Believe me, Frannie, I'm very well-qualified to do you."

I glare at him, but that's only to hide the fact that my entire body is tingling. A reaction to not only his use of my nickname, but also from his slow inspection. A fact which has well and truly fired my very famous temper. Because this man is annoying, and I definitely don't want to be attracted to him. Really.

But apparently, I'm walking proof that you don't always get what you want because, yeah. I'm attracted. Very attracted.

Which means my new goal is to keep that little factoid to myself.

Fortunately, I'm saved from having to come up with a cutting-yet-flirty comeback by the sharp chime of my phone. I frown, irritated that I forgot to put it on silent, then suck in a sharp breath when I see the text message. "*Fucker*," I mutter, then silence the thing and shove it down into my purse.

"What was that about?"

"It's nothing."

He hits the brakes at a red light, then turns to face me. "Fight with a friend or a shitty contract negotiation?"

"No. Nothing like that."

"Then tell me," he demands.

"Excuse me? It's really none of your—"

"Isn't it?"

I start to snap that being harassed by irritating reporters isn't something I'm keen to share, then wince as the truth smashes into me with the force of a wrecking ball. "I'm an idiot," I say.

"Is that so? Want to tell me why?"

I don't, but considering I hired him for this very thing, I suppose I need to. "There's a reporter who's been trying to get me to talk to him," I admit. "About some stuff that happened a long time ago."

"And you said no." His voice is flat. Even.

"It's not about me. He wanted to talk about my best friend from when I was a kid." I feel my throat thicken as the memories come back. "She—she died. It was horrible. All over the news. They interviewed me back then, and it's not something I want to dredge up for some bullshit *Bright Eyes* reboot article."

"Why aren't you signing on for that?" he asks, pulling into the driveway of an adorable little duplex. "I thought you and Aaron went way back."

"You know about that?" Aaron had been a green production assistant on the *Bright Eyes* set when I first met him, and by the time I left the show, he'd worked his way up to being an exec at the studio, overseeing not only *Bright Eyes*, but a dozen other shows in various stages of development.

Now that he's joined the Hollywood elite with Freeway Flix, he's working to develop a reboot of the show that had launched both our careers. And, yeah, he wants me to be part of it.

I'd rather eat glass.

"Why?" Simon asks when I tell him that I turned down Aaron's very generous offer to have me onboard for at least the first season.

I shrug, then look out my window. "I've moved on. Not keen on going backwards."

"And?"

I snap my back straight as I whip around to face him, hating him for being so damn perceptive. "And nothing. My career, my choices."

He doesn't react, but I can feel him studying my face. I stay completely still, forcing myself not to explode. Not to lay into him and demand to know who the hell he thinks he is.

"So that's why the reporter's been bugging you? He wants to know why you're not working on the reboot? Why not just talk to him? Tell him you're in a different place in your career and be done with it."

I push open my car door. "You were hired to protect me. Not to do media intervention." I slide out, then peer back inside, meeting those eyes that are looking back at me, flat and expressionless. Like he knows everything inside me but is determined not to let it show. "Stick with what you know," I snap, then slam the car door.

He's out of his side in an instant, then cocks his head sharply, indicating that I should follow him to the door. I do, then step inside when he opens it and ushers me in. The place is small, I'd guess twelve hundred square feet, with a tiny entrance hall that opens onto a living area that flows into a combination kitchen and dining area. Moving boxes are stacked behind a sofa that faces a media center with a television, sound system, and shelves for vinyl, CDs, DVDs, and books.

A sliding glass door leads to a small backyard, and I can see a tiled patio that leads to a grassy area with a hammock. The whole thing is enclosed by a stone fence.

"It's cute," I say, then nod at the boxes. "Did you just move in?"

"A few months ago. My place in Chicago is on the market."

I take a seat at the small, round dining table. "So you're new to LA?"

"Newly returned," he says. "Born in New York. My mother dragged me here when I was twelve. I bought this place when I turned twenty. I planned to stay, but—well, I didn't live here long. Started traveling, got into security. Ended up in Chicago working for Devlin Saint—he's a friend of Damien and Ryan's. So I turned this place into a rental. Now I figure it can be home base."

I'm an expert at watching faces and listening to voices more than actual words. What I see and hear is pain, and I want to ask him. But that's personal. And personal isn't where I should be going with this guy.

So instead, I say, "It's a great place."

He scoffs.

"What?"

"We're staying here tonight, princess."

I bristle at the harsh tone. And the fact that I don't understand where it came from. "I thought we were going back to my place."

"Changed my mind. Sorry if the house is below your standards. Coffee?" He doesn't wait for me to reply, just heads to the coffee maker and starts to fill the carafe with water. "I don't have a fancy espresso machine. You'll have to deal with Mr. Coffee."

Now I don't just bristle. I'm ramrod straight and one hundred percent pissed off. "What the *fuck* is your problem?"

He shoots me a hard look over his shoulder, then goes back to what he's doing.

"Are you irritated because I said I like this place? One compliment and you morph into an ass? Oh, wait. You were already an ass."

"Compliment? Try condescending pat on the head."

"No. That's not—"

"I mean, I know it's not like your castle, and I'm sorry to make you go slumming, but I think it's the best thing for the night, just in case we were followed. Better to stick for a bit, and I promise you, the security at this place is at least as good as what Mario just installed. It may not look like much, but I assure you it's as safe as your fortress."

"Fuck you," I say. "And fine. I'll sleep on the couch. For your information, you sanctimonious ass, I *do* like this place. It reminds me of the first house I bought when I finally—*finally*—moved out of Beverly Hills and that ridiculous cake-topper of a house my dad had me trapped in."

"Trapped?" He puts down the carafe and looks at me. "In your fancy child star life?"

"Fuck. You." I stand up, wishing I could just walk away from this guy. From his comments and questions and bullshit assumptions about some shiny perfect childhood, when the reality is I always felt like a prisoner in my own damn life.

But that's not something I talk about, and now this bastard is painting some damned rosy picture, and because I was too stupid to insist that Ryan assign Leah, I'm stuck like glue to Mr. Holier Than Thou because someone is trying to kill me, and I really don't know how—

Fuck.

My heart is racing and the world has gone blurry, and I realize I'm looking at him through tears. I push back the chair, then move the short distance to the couch. I kick off my shoes, then settle into the corner, my feet curled under me. There's an olive green throw pillow, and I pull it close, then hug it tight to my chest. *Fuck, fuck, fuck.*

I do *not* show vulnerability, and I do not cry in public. Not ever.

And yet here I am, about to lose it to a waterfall of tears and sobs in front of this utter and complete a-hole, and I don't know if it's because he brought up my dad or because he's a jerk or because I'm just plain scared.

"Frannie…" He's standing at the end of the sofa looking down at me, his face full of contrition.

"It's Francesca," I snap. "Just leave me alone."

He frowns, then sits on the opposite end of the sofa.

I start to get up—if nothing else, I can find the bathroom, lock the door, and hide alone in there. But he puts his hand lightly on my knee.

"Hey," he says.

I want to slap it away. Hell, I want to run away.

Instead, the tears start to fall, and right then all I really want to do is sink into these cushions and disappear.

"Francesca," he says, "I'm sorry." It's that gentle voice that does me in. I can feel the band inside me that's been holding everything. It's tight, stretched to the limit, and now it just snaps, and all the words inside me come flying out, my voice hard and harsh and full of tears.

"I have done nothing—*nothing*—to give you reason to be such a goddamn prick to me, and every time I think that maybe you're going to be just a tiny bit human, you prove me wrong. But I've let you under my skin. I've hired you. Hell, I've *trusted* you. And then you go and slash me with a knife. So you tell me, Simon. Why are you here? Why are you the one protecting me when as far as I can tell, you couldn't care less if I live or die. *Why, why, why?*"

Chapter Six

Simon forced himself not to cringe.

He had no idea what had actually set her off. Something more than the fact that he'd basically called her a spoiled child star, that was for sure. Not his most shining moment, but he knew damn well she'd been called worse in the tabloids.

It wasn't that.

But damned if he knew what the real trigger was.

Right now, though, it didn't matter. At the core of it, he'd lit the fuse.

He was an ass, just like she'd said, and he'd been baiting and belittling her since the moment he'd met her. He'd put his own shit between them, and it had sat there like a ticking time bomb until it had finally exploded.

But, dammit, he wasn't letting his shit destroy her. Frannie was too damn strong, and he wasn't going to be the one who broke her.

"I'm sorry," he said, reaching tentatively to put his hand back on her knee. "I'm really sorry. It's not you."

She released the pillow long enough to slap his hand away. "Screw you," she said. "You think you're so much better than me. You think all I do is playacting. That you're out there saving people and making the world safe for democracy, and that what I do doesn't matter. But you're wrong. My work matters, too. I give people an escape. I give them empathy."

She drew a breath, and he almost started to speak, but she continued on, her words coming out like the rat-a-tat of a machine gun.

"I give them something to talk about, to bond about. And sometimes I even save lives, too. And maybe you don't believe me, but I can remember the name of every girl who wrote me a letter after I did a TV movie about anorexia when I was eighteen. And do you know how many suicide centers had an increase in calls—in *saves*—after one of my television movies back in the day aired? Do you have any idea at all how many people write me to say that they saw themselves in one of my characters? Who thank me for playing a character who got through the bad stuff and was stronger at the end? Do you have any idea—any fucking idea—of how much that can impact people?"

He swallowed, his mouth dry. He didn't want to have this conversation. But he had to. If nothing else, he owed her that.

So he drew in a breath, released it, and said, very simply, "No."

"Then you need to just shut—"

"But I know the other side of it," he said, then hurried on when he saw the fury on her face. "I know the other side too damn well, and I'm sorry, okay? But there's nothing grand or heroic about what I've seen. No lives saved, just lives and households destroyed chasing this fucking dream of Hollywood."

Her expression was tight. Her eyes cold and appraising. She looked ready to bite his head off. But all she said was, "Tell me."

He closed his eyes, wishing he could take the last hour back. Hell, wishing he'd told Damien and Ryan to let Leah take this case and run with it. But he didn't. And somehow, that one simple choice had led him here. To this moment he wanted to avoid but knew he had to face.

"I was born in New York," he said, looking at his hands and not at her face. "When I was six, my mom left my dad for an actor. My dad was ex-military, and he'd moved into private security. He wanted custody, and my mom didn't argue. She was too happy fucking her fake daytime TV doctor to care what happened to me."

He glanced up, saw that she was listening, then looked away again before the confusion—and the sympathy—in her eyes cut straight into his gut. "My dad died on a job. Trying to rescue a little girl from a kidnapper, and it all went down wrong. Three men lost, and the kidnapper, too. But the little girl was safe. My dad died in the hospital. He told me he was sorry, but he didn't regret it. That he'd rescued that girl. That his life had value."

"And your mother's didn't."

Simon shrugged. "She cheated and then left. I don't suppose he'd think anything else."

"But that's what you think, too. That's why you started doing this. Security. Protection."

His chest tightened. He'd almost forgotten she was there, he'd been so wrapped up in those horrible memories. He drew a breath, then met her eyes and nodded.

"My mom got custody of me, of course, and she followed loverboy to LA. They got married. She quit her job—she was a fund manager. I didn't understand what that meant back then, but I knew she was good at her job. She ended up being his manager. Not that it went anywhere. He got one or two tiny roles. We lived in a hovel, and both of them ignored me. I was something to be dealt with. I wasn't her child. I was an inconvenience that had to be managed in order to get to the job. But there was never any job."

He closed his eyes as if he could ward off the rest of the memories, but they just kept coming.

"He started to blame my mother. Started to beat her. I was thirteen then and tried to fight back. He bloodied me up good. Then he…"

"Simon?"

His closed his eyes, wanting to say that she was the last person he wanted to tell this to, because how the hell could she understand? But when he opened his eyes, he saw the compassion on her face and felt himself melting. "He killed her."

"I'm so sorry." She pushed the pillow aside, then leaned forward to take his hand.

"He came after me. I ran. And when I came back with the cops—he was dead, too. That selfish bastard was so lost in the goddamn Hollywood game that he killed himself and my mother when he couldn't make it. And she was too much of a fool to see what he really was."

Her fingers tightened around his. "It wasn't your fault."

The words felt hard. Wrong. He knew they were true, and yet it didn't change the fact that this town—that goddamn business—had destroyed his entire world. And not just the one time, because there was Kristen, too, and—

He shook himself. "I have issues with your industry. I know it. I'm sorry. I took it out on you, and that was a shitty thing to do."

For a moment, he was certain she was going to lash out again. After all, Frannie's temper was famous. But all she said was, "I get it. A lot of folks have been burned by the industry. Me included."

"But you came out the other side unscathed and famous with your perfect life, living large in LaLa Land."

Her eyes darted to the side, but he caught the glimmer of a tear and once again regretted his words.

"I wouldn't go so far as that," she said. "I have fame and money, but

I don't have—" She started to tug her hand away, but he tightened his grip.

"What?"

"Nothing. I have everything, just like you said. Believe me, I'm not complaining."

No, she wasn't. But she wasn't telling him the truth, either. His chest constricted, and he heard himself asking, "Do you want to talk about it?"

"About what? My climb up the ranks to my perfect Hollywood life? Why bother? Or do you think my past is coming back to threaten me?"

"I think that's pretty damn likely, yeah. But I thought you might want to unload. Sometimes it helps. I just learned that the hard way."

She looked up at him, her eyes warm and intense on his, and in that moment, he wanted nothing more than to pull her close and kiss her.

No.

No way was he going there.

For one thing, he had no fucking idea where *that* impulse had come from.

More important, he was on a job. And even if he was warming up to her a tiny bit, there was no way in hell he was sliding down that slippery slope with an actress.

Then she blinked, and the moment passed, leaving Simon wondering if he'd just imagined it. "Well," she said, "I'm glad talking about it helped."

"It did. Thank you." Once again, thoughts of Kristen filled his head. Once again, he pushed them away. It was one thing to dredge up his childhood. He didn't need to dredge her up, too.

Frannie pulled her hand away, then hugged the pillow again.

"I'm a good listener," he told her.

She looked at him with that famous half-smile, then shook her head. "I believe you. But I really don't want to talk about it."

"I get that. I don't know what *it* is. But this reporter does. So I'd say the odds are good that he's the one making the threat. If that's the case, then I need to know. It's a hell of a lot harder to keep you safe if I don't know all the facts."

"I know. But—"

"Hey," he said, conjuring a smile. "I showed you mine. You show me yours."

As he'd hoped, she laughed, and in that moment, he knew why she'd become a star. The sound sparkled, filling the room like the tingle of electricity after a lightning storm.

That's what she was. A force of nature. And the truly baffling thing was that he liked her. Despite her holier-than-thou attitude when they'd met, and despite his stepfather and his mother and all the bullshit with Kristen, he actually liked her.

A good thing, since he was protecting her. But he needed to keep his head.

Because even though he liked her, he knew damn good and well that he could never, ever trust her.

Chapter Seven

I have to give Simon credit for not pushing me.

"I don't want to talk about it now," I'd said. "I know it will help you keep me safe—I really do. And I'll tell you tomorrow after the conference. I'm only on deck in the morning. We can leave by lunch, and I'll tell you everything. I just need..." I'd sucked in a lungful of air and tried to keep the tears at bay. "I've never talked about it since—well, in a really long time. And I try not to think about it. I just need a little time. Please? Please can I have a little time?"

For a moment, I thought he was going to say no. To tell me that he had to know. That it was the only way he could do his job. But he didn't say that. Instead, he'd nodded, then said, "It's okay. I've got your back."

I've got your back.

That was over two hours ago, and I'm still holding his words close as I'm tucked up in the guest bedroom. Because the truth is, I can't remember the last time it felt like anyone truly had my back. My agent, maybe. But that's her job. Other than that? Well, I've been pretty much flying solo for years.

I think of Carolyn, my childhood bestie, and squeeze my eyes shut. I hate this. The memories that stupid reporter is dredging up. The note that's probably just bullshit but gets me in the gut. Fear and anger and betrayal.

And secrets. Always secrets.

I'm surprised that I genuinely want to tell Simon tomorrow. I've held on to these secrets too long, and I don't know how to let go. But knowing that Simon will catch me...that feels pretty damn nice.

I don't realize that I've gotten out of bed. I'm tired—mentally and physically exhausted—but my body has other plans, and before I realize it, I'm in my robe and at the door. I hesitate, then push it open, walking the short distance from my guest room to the master bedroom at the end of the hall. I'm hoping the door is open a crack—I can't tell in the dim lighting—because then it's like permission to go inside.

But it's not. It's closed tight, though I don't know if it's locked or not.

I want to turn the knob and find out, but that's going too far. I hesitate, letting the thought settle. With any other man, I wouldn't even pause. I'd just turn the knob, go inside, and get into his bed. I know what I want, after all, and I'm more than comfortable taking charge.

I close my hand around the knob, telling myself I should do just that. I'm naked beneath the robe, and I close my eyes, feeling my body respond to the thought of finding him there. Of letting the robe fall off my shoulders. Of sliding under the covers with him, my hand closing around his cock as my lips find his.

Of taking what I want, just like I always have, then snuggling up close and telling him my secrets.

I have a reputation for seducing my co-stars, after all, so I know I can do this. I can make him hot. Make him hard. And it doesn't have to mean anything.

I never go after a co-star who's involved, because I don't believe in fucking up someone else's relationship. But there's an intimacy in working together on a film, and being intimate in bed just helps that relationship. That trust.

Which is what I tell them, but it's bullshit.

The truth is I like being in control. I like knowing that I'm the one taking the lead. I'm the one doing the seducing. Because if that's the case, then I'm not the one getting hurt.

Except that's not what I want now. Not with Simon. I don't want to be the one pushing and taking and claiming. I want to be the one who surrenders.

That word comes back to me. What he'd said at my house. That one simple word that had pissed me off even as much as it had turned me on, even though he hadn't been talking about sex at all.

Obey.

I shiver, my nipples tightening, my whole body suddenly aware. I close my hand on the knob again, but I don't turn. I can't—I won't—be the one who pushes. Not with him. Not the first time.

I fully intend to head back to my own room, but somehow I don't end up there. Instead, I go to the back door, then look out at the dark night, illuminated only by the dim glow from a partial moon.

I don't even realize I've opened the door until I'm outside, the air warm around me. I sigh, then step off the patio so that my bare feet are in the thick, trimmed grass. I lean back against the post and close my eyes, the grass beneath me and the sky above me, and Simon in the house looking over me.

I feel safe. Taken care of. And that's not a feeling I'm used to.

I want him.

I want him, but I need to stop. He's my bodyguard. He's here to protect me. But he doesn't want me. I'm not even sure he likes me, though we've at least reached a détente.

So I need to stop thinking like that because I don't need the frustration, and I need to just get the fuck over it.

I'm about to push away from the post and head back inside to bed when I feel a hand on my shoulder. I start to cry out, but another hand closes over my mouth, and in that instant, I know just how badly I screwed up. I'd been safe in his house, but out here—out under the sky—I'm a target, and I—

"You shouldn't be out here."

My entire body goes limp with relief, and I draw in a breath as he removes his hand from my mouth.

"I know. I'm sorry. I wasn't thinking." I tense, readying myself for the verbal lashing as he tells me what an idiot I was.

But that's not what he says. Instead, he says, "Why didn't you come in?"

"What—"

"I heard you outside my room," he says. "I could practically feel your desire. But you walked away."

I want to tell him he's wrong. That he's too damn arrogant for his own good.

Except he's not wrong at all, and right then, I can barely form words, much less think clearly.

He's still behind me, my head against the post. He trails his hands down my arms, then stops near my waist. Before I even realize his hands have moved, he's holding the sash. "Your call, sweetheart," he whispers, his voice soft near my ear. I should say no. I should tell him this is unprofessional and we can't go there.

I should tell him I don't want him at all.

Instead, I say, "Yes. Oh, yes, please."

I hear his low, sensual growl as he opens the robe, then I whimper as his hands stroke my skin, his fingers slipping lower until he's stroking the juncture between my sex and my thigh, and I'm going crazy, desperate to feel him against my clit. Desperate for his fingers—his cock—to be deep inside me.

Then his hands are gone, and he's standing in front of me. "Simon," I beg. "Please."

He moves closer, then opens the robe more so that my breasts are completely exposed. His gaze roams over me, slow and easy, as if he's assessing where to touch me. How to make me melt. And I want to. Dear God, I want to melt.

"Touch yourself," he says.

My eyes go wide. "What?"

"Your fingers. Your breasts. Your pussy."

I shiver from the heat in his words. "Simon…"

"Either obey me or say no, and we stop right now. Those are your only choices."

I bite my lip, but I also close my eyes as I slip my fingers between my legs, then gasp when I brush my clit, and my whole body sparks.

"Oh, baby," he says, his hands going to my hips. "Keep your eyes closed."

"Okay."

"Excuse me?"

I fight a smile, remembering the way he'd ordered me to obey him. And the way it had turned me on even as it pissed me off.

Right now, it only turned me on. "Yes, sir."

"Better," he says, his tongue teasing my navel. "Put your hands on your breasts. Play with your nipples. And spread your legs for me."

I do, more turned on than I've ever been. Never once have I let a man take so much control, and it's everything I can do not to cry out as his hands slide around to cup my ass and his tongue teases my clit. I lean back, surrendering. Ready to let him do anything and everything. Willing to let him completely own me.

As if he can read my thoughts, he says, "I spent some time reading about you. About how you fuck your co-stars. How you seduce them. Is it true?"

"Mostly, yes."

"Why?"

"I like being in control," I admit.

"Who's in control now?"

"You are." My voice is little more than a breath.

"And do you like it?"

"God, yes."

"Should I stop? Should I surrender to you?"

I reach out and grab his hair, my voice almost panicky as I say, "No. Please, Simon, no."

"And the alcohol? The drugs? There are stories about you getting drunk and passing out in a hot tub. That's dangerous stuff." His fingers thrust deep inside me, and I groan, arching back as I grind against his hand. "A hell of a lot more dangerous than I am."

"It's not true," I say, barely managing to get the words out.

"Don't lie to me. Never lie to me."

"I'm not. It never happened. I—I'm careful, and I don't do drugs. We'd been filming, and I was exhausted. I fell asleep in the hot tub, but that was all. And someone posted a picture, and the rumor got started."

"And you let it go."

"Yes," I whisper, my hips moving. I want more. I want the explosion. I want *him.*

"You're not as wild as you like people to think. You're playing the game. You've played it your whole life."

"Yes."

"You don't get to play it with me."

There's an edge to his voice, and I open my eyes. He's looking up at me, and it's more than just desire I see there. "So this isn't a game?" I whisper.

He doesn't answer. Instead, he bends forward, his tongue teasing my clit as his fingers find my G-spot. I writhe against him, that pressure building. My nipples going tight, my body going tense as the explosion comes closer and closer and closer until—

He pulls away, and I hear myself whimper.

He stands, then kisses me, his hand cupping my sex. "Goodnight, Frannie," he whispers, and his use of my nickname again after I'd snapped at him has me melting even more.

His lips brush my ear. "And no finishing yourself off." He pulls back to meet my eyes. "Obey," he says, then heads back inside, leaving me hot and needy and desperately wanting him.

Chapter Eight

He liked her.

No, not just *like*. He actually respected her.

More than that, he was attracted to her. *Attracted*. Wasn't that a lame word. It was more than attraction. It was primal. It was need. He wanted to possess her. To claim her. To wrap her in his arms and keep her safe and close and *his*.

And if that wasn't the damnedest, most bizarre thing ever…

Simon shook his head, trying to clear those crazy thoughts. Frannie had turned out to not be the bitch from hell that he'd expected. Great. Good.

And, yes, he was attracted to her—something that was clearly mutual, and something that he was more than willing to pursue, especially now that he'd tasted her. Had felt her responsiveness. Her need.

Her trust.

He'd told her to obey, and she had. This woman who'd lived her life and her career by grabbing control. With him, she'd surrendered, almost without question.

It was humbling. Surprising.

And one hell of a turn-on.

But love?

No way.

Lust. It was lust. And so long as it was mutual, what was the harm in pursuing it?

He pushed the thoughts away as he watched her interacting with her fans. They'd been at the con now for almost four hours. She'd been on two panels, after which she'd chatted with anyone who'd come up until the con organizers had kicked them out of the room for the next event.

Now they were in the hotel basement, the only place she could find where the fans could come, and they'd be out of the way of other panels and events. The line was huge, but Frannie had promised all the fans that she'd stay and sign autographs for everyone. A few wanted to ask about her other work, but most were there because of her Blue Zenith superhero movies. Films that Simon knew meant far less to her than her smaller passion projects like the upcoming *Spiraling*.

But while the Blue Zenith movies might mean less to her, it was clear that the fans didn't. She didn't simply sign her name to a proffered program. Instead, she talked with each person, even the ones who were too shy to start the conversation themselves.

Every fan left with a smile and a memory to be cherished, and it was all because Frannie cared. She was, in a word, nice.

And Simon was surprised to realize that he wasn't surprised at all. Before this assignment, he would have laid money that she blew off her fans, barely deigning to scrawl her name when they asked for an autograph, more often just lifting her nose and ignoring them.

Now he knew the real woman, not the celebrity bitch he'd concocted in his mind and not the controlling femme fatale that the press chattered on about. She knew how to grab control, sure, but that was self-preservation.

The bottom line was that she respected the fans. And they loved her for it.

Hell, maybe he did, too.

The thought slammed hard against him, and he tried to push it away. But the harder he tried, the more it clung to him. *Love?*

No way. Respect, sure. Like, absolutely.

But love?

No way.

Or at least, not yet.

"You hanging in there?"

Simon looked up to see Trevor approaching with two Styrofoam cups of coffee. Stark Security had sent a team, of course, and Leah and Jasper were on the other side of the open area, both wearing blue jackets with SECURITY stenciled on the back. He'd hoped that Renly would be working today—after all, he'd once dated Frannie back in his Hollywood stunt coordinator days—and Simon would have loved to hear Renly's thoughts on her.

Now he turned to Trevor. "Thanks," he said, taking the coffee. "So do you know Frannie? Damien and Ryan said something about you being too known in this world to play her fake boyfriend."

Trevor's brows raised. "Is that what you are? A fake boyfriend?"

"Excuse me?"

The other man shrugged. "I've been watching you all day, my friend. There's some serious sparks flying between the two of you. Either you're as good an actor as Frannie is, or something's going on."

Simon sighed. "Would that be bad? You know her, right? So tell me. How much trouble will I be in if I let her under my skin?"

"Seems to me it's a little too late to be asking that."

Simon scowled; Trevor wasn't wrong. "Are you going to give me grief or answer the question?" He glanced at the line of fans. Only a few left, which meant he only had a few moments to get answers.

"Frannie's a good egg," Trevor said. "My aunt's been in the industry for years. She's a script supervisor, and she's worked on a lot of films with Frannie, and she was on the crew for *Bright Eyes*, too."

"Frannie's break-out show."

"She always laughs when there's stuff in the news that suggests Frannie is a stuck-up bitch. She says she believes the sex stuff—Frannie seducing her co-stars. I guess the woman's got control issues."

"That she does."

"But the stuff about Frannie being a bitch in general? No way. Says she's as professional as they come." He cocked his head. "Want to tell me why you're asking?"

"Nope."

Trevor laughed. "Good luck. I get the impression she's a handful. I also think she's probably worth the effort."

"Thanks. And thanks for hanging. Weren't you supposed to be off an hour ago? I thought you were meeting a friend. Going to go be an attendee at the con. Not just a working guy."

"Nah, it's fine. Turns out he's running late."

"Date?"

"I wouldn't kick him out of my bed. But, no. He's straight and just a friend. Ollie McKee."

"The FBI agent," Simon said, remembering meeting the man who was a lifelong friend of Damien's wife, Nikki. "He had that on-again-off-again engagement for a while, right?"

"Yeah. Before we met, but yeah. I heard about that."

Simon shrugged. "Maybe he's ready to move on to you."

"Don't tease me, man."

"Just saying, maybe it's time you found out for sure."

Trevor shot him a sideways glance. "I'm serious. Drop it. He's a good friend. That's important to me."

"Right. Sorry. I didn't mean to push. Or pry." Hell, he had relationships on the brain. Or at least, he had Frannie on the brain. He'd taken a hell of a risk last night. He'd already decided that he wanted her in his life, but last night...?

Last night raised the question of how. More than casual friends, that was for sure, and it seemed she wanted that, too. But a relationship?

He didn't do relationships with actresses. That was his longstanding rule, and for damn good reason.

So that left friends. Or more specifically, friends with benefits.

And that was fine by him. Hell, that was perfect.

Except if it was so damn perfect, then why did it feel so wrong?

* * * *

"Ms. Muratti! Francesca!"

They were heading across the hotel lobby toward the elevators that led to the parking garage when Simon heard the voice. He took Frannie's hand, moving in front of her as they turned around to see the pale blond man in jeans and a flannel shirt hurrying toward them.

Beyond the man, he saw Aaron and Matthew walking together. Aaron looked up, and for a moment, Simon was certain he was going to come over. Then he returned his attention to Matthew, and the two of them cut off to the right, veering away from him and Frannie in favor of the food court.

"That's him," Frannie said. "The reporter."

"Thank you," the man said, breathing hard as he caught up to them. "Thank you."

They were on a bridge that connected the two sections of the hotels. The walls were glass, looking down on the street below, and Simon lunged forward, taking the reporter by the collar and slamming him back up against one. "You sent that note?"

"I—I—it's just that I needed corroboration."

The guy was so agitated, it was a wonder he didn't piss himself. He glanced at Frannie, who nodded. Then he released the guy and took a step back. "Talk," he said. "And if I don't like what I hear, it's not going to go well for you."

"I'm sorry. I know the note was stupid. Really. But I just—I didn't know what to do. I'm sitting on a career-making story, but my source is dead. I can't do a thing with this story without corroboration."

"Why the hell is that my problem?" Frannie asked.

"Because you're the only one alive who can help me."

"I—" She cut herself off with a shake of her head.

"Here," Simon said, then led them both into the stairwell, hoping to avoid the curious stares—and possible keen hearing—of the fans who were passing them on the bridge, their eyes on Frannie.

"What's your name?" Simon asked. "Let's start there."

"Corey. Corey Burnet."

"Good start. Now what's the story?" Simon asked. "What story is so damn important that you're willing to send threatening notes and risk being arrested in order to maybe get corroboration?"

The reporter winced, and Simon was certain that the idiot had pulled a stupid prank designed to get Frannie to talk. But there was no legitimate threat. *Idiot.*

"It's okay, Frannie," he said, putting his hand on the small of her back. "This guy's not going to hurt you, are you?"

"You son-of-a-bitch," she said. "Do you have any idea how scared I was?"

"I'm sorry. I'm so sorry. I just—it's just, this could be really important. This could be huge. And there are dangerous people who don't want this published. But it needs to be. Please, please believe me that it needs to be."

"You sent me a threat. You threatened my life, and you didn't even tell me why."

The pale reporter looked like he was about to cry. He was probably in his early thirties, but right then, he looked all of 12. "I'm sorry. It was stupid. I'm sorry. But if you would only let me tell you—"

"Then talk," Simon said. "We're standing here, we're listening. Talk. And it better be good."

"Okay. Right. Okay." He cleared his throat. "So I've always been fascinated by Hollywood scandals. It's kind of what I write about. I started out in high school writing about scandals that happened on movie sets. And then when I actually got a job in LA, it was like the biggest deal ever for me."

"We don't need your life story, Burnet. Cut to the chase."

"Yeah, okay. Right. Carolyn Pruitt," he said, and in his peripheral vision, Simon saw Frannie hug herself. "That was such a huge story, right? And no one ever really knew the whole story."

He did a mental sweep of his research on Frannie, then remembered that Carolyn Pruitt had been a minor recurring character on her first show, *Bright Eyes*. Carolyn's father had been the show's producer, Anthony Pruitt, and they'd both died on one horrible night almost twenty years ago.

"Go on," Simon said, reaching out to take Frannie's hand, relieved when she held it tight.

"Yeah, right. Um, so as I'm sure both of you know, Carolyn and her father were killed in her bedroom one night when she was fifteen."

"That bastard was abusing her," Frannie said. Simon saw tears in her eyes. "You damn well better have something new to tell me, because this is not something I want to be revisiting." She sniffed, then swiped a tear away. "He used to hit on me, too, if that's the kind of corroboration you're looking for. I didn't know until after the fact that he'd touched her like that. I—I thought about some of our conversations and realized. But I never knew at the time."

Tears were falling freely now, and Simon squeezed her hand. "It wasn't your fault," he said.

She looked at him as if he'd just told the biggest lie imaginable. "I should have known."

"What happened?" he asked gently.

"Apparently her mom—Leslie—walked in when Pruitt was trying to—Leslie lost her shit and killed them both." Her throat was clogged, the words barely able to come out.

"That was the story," Burnet said. "But there's more to it."

Her head snapped up, and her voice was hard and tight when she asked, "What are you talking about?"

"You know that her mom was convicted. That they found a gun on her, and everyone believed that she shot him, then herself. But she survived."

Frannie's hand tightened around Simon's fingers. "Go on."

"She pled guilty by reason of insanity and ended up in a facility. Recently, she was allowed to move to an assisted living community. I interviewed her there. She told me that there was someone else there that night. She said that she did walk in to Carolyn's bedroom, and she saw Carolyn trying to fight off Pruitt. Pruitt shoved her back, and he slammed her head hard against the wall. She passed out."

Frannie was squeezing Simon's hand so hard he was surprised that the bones didn't crunch. He wanted to ask her what was going on in her head, but Burnet barreled on.

"According to Leslie, Pruitt freaked out. He started to shake Carolyn. Saying he hadn't meant to hurt her. And then she came to. She'd only been knocked out."

"What?" Frannie looked between Simon and the reporter, her face ghostly pale. "He revived her?"

"That's what the mom said," Burnet confirmed. "She was in this weird little alcove that separated Carolyn's room from the main hallway. The room had double doors that opened onto the pool, and I guess that's how Carolyn wanted everyone to come and go. So she had furniture and stuff in the other entrance way. Mostly blocked. But it was still useable. And Leslie was standing there, mostly hidden in the shadows."

"Carolyn was alive?" Frannie had spoken the words, but her voice didn't sound like hers. She sounded lost. Alone. And terribly, terribly sad.

"Yeah. And Leslie was about to run to her daughter, but then someone else came into the room."

"*What? Who?*"

"I can't say. That's the part I need you to corroborate. But he started screaming that Carolyn was a slut. That she belonged to him. That he'd always known that she was pulling strings, trying to climb her way up the acting ladder by fucking her stepfather."

"That's stupid," Frannie said. "Carolyn didn't even want to be an actress. She was only in the show because her stepfather wanted her to be."

"I'm just telling you what her mom told me."

"So then what happened?"

"The guy came in, and he shot Pruitt in the back of the head. Then he went over to Carolyn, and he told her he loved her, and he told her that she'd betrayed him, and he smacked her head against the wall once again. That time, he killed her." The guy swallowed, took a deep breath. "Leslie must have made a sound, because he found her. She tried to get away, but she tripped, and the guy caught her. He put the gun in her hand, then fired it toward Pruitt. He wanted gunpowder on her fingers."

"Oh, God," Frannie said, and Simon realized that he'd pulled her close. No longer just holding her hand, but holding her.

"Then he made her turn the gun on herself and fire again into her face. After that, he ran, probably assuming she'd die. She almost did. She lost an eye and some motor function. But she survived."

"And she was convicted," Frannie said, her voice thin. "She didn't do it, but she was convicted."

"I know. I'm sorry."

"I should go see her. All these years..." She trailed off with a shudder. "I should go see her."

"You can't," Burnet said. "She's dead."

"Oh." Frannie closed her eyes, then drew a deep breath. "From her injuries?"

"Suicide. Got her hands on something. Sleeping pills, I guess. Drowned in her bathtub. She had a small unit at the facility."

"I'm so, so sorry to hear that. I was close to Carolyn, but not her mom. I mean, I knew her, but only a little, but this is horrible."

Simon put his arm around her waist and pulled her close, relishing the easy way she leaned into him, letting him comfort her.

"What exactly is it you need, Mr. Burnet?" Simon asked.

"Corroboration of Leslie's story. About who really killed Carolyn. And who really shot Pruitt and Leslie."

Frannie shook her head as she met Simon's eyes. He saw the confusion there. "I don't understand. I don't know anything."

"Leslie said you might."

"*What?*" Frannie pulled away from him, then took a step forward. "What are you talking about?"

"Leslie said you were there, too. She saw you walk past her window. She said you did it all the time. You would go visit Carolyn at night. The two of you would hang out in her room. She never closed the curtains all the way because she liked to look at the hills. And every night that you came over, she'd see you."

Frannie dropped Simon's hand. "I need you to go," she said to Burnet.

"Please. I need corroboration. If you were there, then you must have seen the other person. The one who framed Carolyn's mom. Who slammed Carolyn's head against the wall the second time, killing her? I'm only looking for corroboration. I know who it is. Leslie told me. All you have to do is tell me that you know, too. Give me a name, and I will publish this story and take down the killer who murdered your best friend. Tell me. Let me help put this man away."

"It's okay, Frannie," Simon said. "I think you should tell him. It was an asshole move to threaten you, but if you can get justice for Carolyn and Leslie...."

But Frannie was shaking her head, her eyes wide and frightened. "I don't know who it was. I was there. You're right about that. But I didn't see anybody else. No one came in while I was there. It was just me in the shadows. And I was terrified."

Burnet stared at her, looking dejected. Looking as if all he wanted to do was take her by the throat and force the truth out of her. But Simon knew better. Simon believed her. There was nobody else.

Leslie had played a Hail Mary. She'd lost it and screwed up and tried to put the blame on someone else. To make her husband not be an abusive murderer. To make herself not be a killer. But wishing wouldn't change the truth.

"You need to go," Simon said. "She's told you she didn't see anyone else. That's the end of it. You walk right now, we'll forget about your note. But if we hear another word out of you, we'll arrest you in a heartbeat. And I assure you, even though you may not realize it, that threat you sent is actionable. She'll press charges, and you will serve time. Do you understand me?"

Burnet nodded. "I didn't mean to scare you."

"Of course you did," she snapped. "And it worked. But I don't know anything. So you did it for nothing, you son of a bitch. You dredged it all up for nothing."

"I'm sorry," Burnet said, sounding genuinely contrite. Not that it mattered.

"Just get the hell out of here," Simon said, and the reporter turned and scurried away, pushing out of the stairwell door and back into the hubbub of the con.

Frannie looked at Simon, her eyes burning with tears. "Get me to the car," she said, and he took her by the arm and led her down the two levels to the lobby, then into the parking structure until finally they reached his Honda.

As soon as they were inside with the doors closed, her tears started to flow.

"I'm sorry," she said when her body had stopped shaking, and she looked at him through red-rimmed eyes and a face splotchy from crying. "That was the most horrible night of my life," she said.

"Do you want to talk about it?"

"No. Yes. I don't know. I did go," she said, because apparently she did want to talk about it. "I got there, and it was supposed to just be me and Carolyn hanging out that night. But Pruitt was in the room with her. She told me that he used to try to touch her, he did the same to me too, so I never thought that it was more than just stupid touching on set. She'd suggested that it was, but I guess I never really listened. It wasn't until that night that I realized what he really did to her."

"It's not your fault."

"I should have understood that it was worse than what she was really saying." She shook her head. "It doesn't matter now. But I walked in, and

I saw her fighting him off. He slammed her head against the wall. I thought she died. And I was so scared. I made a noise, and he looked in my direction. I thought he'd seen me, so I ran. I ran so fast. I went to the cabana. I was going to hide there. But I realized he'd probably find me. So I left. But I took her diary because now I wanted to read it. I wanted to know if she'd written about what he'd done to her."

"How did you get her diary?"

"She kept it hidden in the cabana. Said she was afraid he'd read her entries. I thought she was paranoid. Now I guess she wasn't."

"So you took it. Then what?"

"I ran down the service drive back to my car. I was sixteen. I'd just started driving. I left, and I went and told my father. I told him we had to go to the police. That the diary had proof that Pruitt had been abusing her for a while. And I wanted the cops to arrest him."

"What did the cops say?" Simon asked. "By the time they got there, Leslie had shot him, right?"

"We didn't go. My dad told me I had to throw the diary away and never say anything. Otherwise I might lose my job, and my dad wouldn't do anything that might keep me from working in the business. He always said if I ever stopped working, we'd starve, because he was my manager, and that meant all we had was my income. And he said if I ever opened my mouth, everyone would look at me and call me a liar, because Pruitt was well respected in the industry."

"Did you get rid of it?"

She shook her head. "No. I told him I did. But I lied. I've kept it all this time. It's all I have left of her."

He took her hand. "Tell me the rest. Tell me about your father."

It was clear she didn't want to. She pulled her hand free, then hugged herself before speaking. "He told me that we couldn't say anything. That I would be dragged through the press and that I would lose my job. That I couldn't say one thing that would sully Pruitt's good name because the scandal might mean they'd cancel *Bright Eyes*."

She drew in a deep breath, then closed her eyes as if gathering courage.

When she opened them again, her expression was fierce. "My mother died when I was little, so I only had my dad. He never beat me, but he was a controlling bastard and verbally abusive. I remember how my skin would feel raw after he lost his temper just from the horrible things he would say. And I obeyed. Always. I think because I was always afraid there'd be a blow coming one day. So I was always the good girl." She swallowed, then blew out a breath. "But this time, I was going to disobey and suffer the consequences."

"What do you mean?"

"That I was going to go to the police anyway. I was—I really was. But then the next morning, the news came out that he was dead, and I figured my dad couldn't argue anymore. So I told him I was going. But then he said that I still couldn't. Because once they learned that I was there, I would be a suspect too. I believed him. I was scared. I was so scared."

"Of course you were. Who wouldn't be?"

"But there *wasn't* anybody else there. I never saw anybody else. They must have come as I was leaving. I just never saw them."

"Did you know that her mother was there?"

"No. Not until it came out that she was the one who shot him." She exhaled a shaky breath. "I lost my friend that day. I just wanted to forget. I tried to forget, but I never did."

He pulled her close and held her. "No. Of course you didn't."

"I'm sorry. I probably should have realized that was what the note was about. It's the biggest scandal of my life. The one I pushed down the hardest. Nothing else compares."

"It's okay. We know now. And it's over."

"So this is it," she said. "This threat against me. It's gone. I don't need a bodyguard anymore."

"No. I don't think you do. It was pretty clear that you had no idea what he was talking about. Plus, I don't think he's dangerous. He sent that note as a stupid maneuver to try to get you to talk, but he would never have followed through."

"I know. He's an idiot. The world is full of idiots."

"Yes. That's true." He twined his fingers with hers, wishing they could stay like that, still and quiet and safe. After a moment, he released her, then started the car. "Come on. I'll take you home."

"And then you'll go?"

He tensed inside. "Job's done. You don't need me to stay." He managed to keep his voice level. To not let her hear the disappointment that surprised even him.

She turned to him then, her teeth grazing her lower lip. "What if I asked you to stay?"

"Why? Do you still need protection?"

"No," she said, squeezing his hand. "But I think... Simon, I think I might need you."

Chapter Nine

I hold my breath, thinking he's going to say nothing. That I'm going to have laid my heart—or at least my desire—on the line, and he's going to spurn me.

Then he kills he engine, and hope fills my chest. When he turns to me, his face is completely expressionless, but his eyes say everything. They show lust and need and desire, and I think that I've won. That I took a risk, and it paid off. He wants me. And oh, dear God, I want him too. More than I ever thought I could want any man.

"I don't date actresses," he says, shattering all of my hope. "I made up my mind a long time ago about that. I already told you about my mother. That was the first brick. The rest came with Kristen. She wanted to be an actress. We were going to get married. Turns out I wasn't as attractive as the sitcom actor she met at class who promised he could get her an audition. She left me. She told me that I couldn't do enough for her. That she had to take care of her craft. That she had to put herself above everything else. So she walked. And she took my heart with her."

"I'm so sorry." I want to kill the bitch because she hurt him and because she destroyed this newly budding thing that's growing between us before it's even had a chance to root.

"Between my mother and my fiancée, I got soured on the industry. Or I got soured by the integrity of the people in it."

"I really am sorry. And I do understand. I would never want you to do something that you don't want to do." I'm trying desperately to be mature and to fight back tears, but I fear I'm going to lose one or both of those battles.

"I don't want to do something I don't want to do either," he says.

Then, to my utter confusion, he leans forward and sweetly kisses me. I taste the tears when I speak. "Is that goodbye?"

"No," he says. "It's thank you. I've held on to that for a long time. That belief that everybody who works in this business is as cold as my mother and my girlfriend. It's not true. Thank you for that."

"Don't put me on a pedestal," I say, even though I should be turning backflips and telling him that yes, yes, I'm the perfect woman. Perfect for him, and to please just take me home and take me to bed. Instead, I find myself saying, "I fucked my way through this town."

"You told me. And I get why. And as far as I can see, you've never pretended to be someone you're not."

"No. I haven't. But I don't know. I feel like I've become hard."

He takes my hand and lifts it to his mouth, gently kissing my knuckles. "You're not. You do a good job wearing your armor, but deep inside, you're not hard at all. Or if you are, maybe we both are. We're a lot alike, you know. We've both gone through this life mostly alone."

I reach for his hand and squeeze. "We don't have to be."

"Frannie." He pulls his hand free, then stands up and starts pacing. "I don't even know if I should say this."

"Please do. It's usually the things left unsaid that cause problems."

"You're right about that." He drags his fingers through his hair. "It's just that this is all so fast. The way I feel about you. The things you make me imagine."

I tilt my head, my entire body filling with happiness. "Naughty things?"

He laughs. "Definitely. But tender things too. Waking up next to you. Walking with you. It's stupid. And it's not."

"No." My voice is thick with lust. "It's not stupid at all."

"Frannie," he says, and there's no denying the heat in his voice. "I want to be inside you," he whispers. "How comfortable are you with that bad girl persona?"

My brows rise as I try to figure out what he's thinking. "I'll be as bad as you want me to be."

"Good. Get out of the car."

"What? Why—"

"Frannie," he says, with a very wicked grin. "Obey."

The word goes straight through me, settling between my thighs, and I do as he says. Less than two minutes later, we're back in the stairwell. I know it's dangerous. There are a zillion people at this con, and the parking garage is full. Anyone could find us. But the air between us is crackling, and the moment he takes my hand, I know that nothing else matters.

He pulls me close, then spins me around until my back is against the wall and his mouth is on mine. I don't even know how he managed it, but he's tugged up my skirt, and his fingers are inside my panties.

I moan as my fingers go to his fly. I want this.

"You're mine," he says. "Only mine."

"Yes," I say as he rips off my panties then shoves them in his pocket. My skirt is up, and he lifts me, his hands cupping my ass as my legs lock around him. His cock is right there, and I'm so damn wet.

"Quiet," he says, then teases his cock at my core. I cling to his shoulders, my hips going forward as my shoulders press against the wall. I'm so wet, but he's torturing me. Going slowly. Stretching me. Filling me.

"Please. Oh, God, please."

And then, with one hard thrust, he's deep inside me. I cry out, but his hand over my mouth silences me. He pounds into me as I shift one hand down to tease my clit and stroke his cock with each thrust.

Our eyes lock, and right then, I feel both lost and found. I feel like I belong.

In that moment when my body tightens around him, I arch back, then swallow a scream as his mouth closes over mine, his teeth nipping my lip and our bodies rocking together. When we finally explode, the force of our joint orgasm is so intense it's a wonder we don't bring the whole damn hotel down on us.

"Wow," I say a few minutes later as we're both sitting on a step, our clothes adjusted back to some semblance of normalcy. "That was great."

"Yeah," he says. "It really was."

I meet his eyes. "Take me home, Simon. Take me home, and let's do it again."

Chapter Ten

"Your bed is huge," Simon said. "It's like you're on a different continent."

They were back at her house after he'd taken her in the stairwell. Wonderful and decadent, and all the more so because of the risk of getting caught.

Exciting, yes, but this was better. Her huge bedroom was dominated by a custom-made bed that she swore had never had another man in it.

"I don't bring men back here," she said. "That's what hotels are for."

"And stairwells?"

She laughed. "I've never done that before either."

"Really?" He didn't know why that was important to him. Probably because he knew she'd had a lot of flings. He wanted something of theirs. Something unshared.

"Really," she said. "I wanted that for us."

"Tell me why."

"Because I want to be yours," she said. "That's why you're in this bed. In my inner sanctum."

She bent forward to kiss him, and he felt his soul sing. Then she peeled off her clothes until she was standing naked in front of him. "Yup. We're in the inner sanctum now." She slid into his arms and wiggled against him, her hand cupping his erection.

He slipped his fingers between her legs. "This is the only inner sanctum I care about right now."

She laughed. "Good answer." Then she lifted herself up and brushed her lips against his ear. "Fuck me, Simon."

"No." The word came out firm, and her eyes went wide. Her nipples tightened, and he saw the flush rise in her skin. "Not until I'm certain that you're ready."

"I am," she assured him, but he shook his head, then ordered her to lie down.

It was only after his mouth and fingers had explored every sweet, delicious inch of her that he finally thrust inside her. Plain old missionary, but it felt like the most mind-blowing sex of his life, and they repeated it not once, but twice, trying other positions. But always face to face. Someday he'd take her from behind. Right now, he wanted to get lost in her eyes when he got lost inside her.

They christened every part of the bed before giving in to exhaustion, and he felt like he'd traveled the world as he'd traveled the woman.

And while the sex had been incredible, it was the connection he felt with Frannie that had truly blown his mind.

It seemed like only five minutes ago, he would have sold his soul to have avoided her. Now he couldn't get enough of her.

"I'm serious," he said, reaching for her and tugging her to him as she giggled and kicked. "This bed is way too big. You're on another planet. I need you down here on earth with me."

"Yeah? And how are you going to keep me here?" She rolled over, then climbed on top of him. He was already hard again, and now his cock teased her ass as she straddled him, her body rocking slowly as she rubbed her clit against his lower abdomen. "You want me to stay on this side of the Atlantic, you need to be more proactive than that."

"Do I?" He slipped his hand between them, his fingers teasing their way inside her as she rubbed her clit on the heel of his hand. She was perfect. Her sense of humor. Her compassion. The way she could take charge or surrender. And, yeah, her body. He knew she paid trainers handsomely to keep her in top shape, but damned if they didn't do a good job. And it wasn't just surface. The woman had strength and stamina. She could damn sure keep up with him.

"Tell me what you want," he whispered as he thrust his fingers deeper inside her.

She arched back, moaning a bit, her hips shifting as if she was trying to find just *that* spot. With his free hand, he reached up for her nipple, then rolled it between his thumb and his forefinger.

"What I want?" she repeated.

"This?" He tightened his grip on her nipple and felt her pussy tighten around his fingers. "Or this?" He slipped his fingers out of her, easing his hand back until he was teasing her ass, and she cried out, begging him to do more than tease.

"Tell me," he demanded, his thumb teasing her pussy as his index finger played with her ass. Her eyes were closed, and the pleasure and need he saw on her face was almost enough to make him come right then.

"I thought I was your toy," she said. "Yours to command. To fuck. To sweetly torture." She bent forward, lifting her ass until his cock was right there. "That's what I want," she said as her breasts rubbed against his chest. "All I want is to be yours. Completely."

He swallowed, his mouth suddenly dry as he met her eyes. The moment felt heavy. Important.

And utterly terrifying.

He lifted a hand to stroke her hair, then held her head in place so she couldn't look away. "Baby, I need to know what you mean. Are we playing sex games or are we—"

"No games," she said. "Not about that." She bit her lip, and he saw her gather her courage, then press on. "I want to see what we can be together. I've never—I've never felt like this, and I don't mean this," she added, wiggling against his cock. "I mean this." She pushed up higher, then held his hand to her heart. "Is it just me?"

"No," he said, meeting her eyes and seeing the future reflected in them. "It's not just you."

"So you'll stay? Even though you don't have to protect me anymore?"

"I'll stay," he said, wanting to get lost in that sweet smile.

"Good," she said. "But Simon, you still have to protect my heart."

"Always," he promised, knowing that was an oath he would willingly die for.

* * * *

The first two days, he told Ryan that he was staying with her just to make sure Burnet believed Frannie and didn't try to harass her for more info.

On the third day, he told Ryan he was taking some personal time after the case.

After a week, he told Ryan that he and Frannie were involved, and since she had a week before shooting began on *Spiraling*, he was taking more time off.

"You haven't been there long enough to have accrued time off," Frannie said, snuggling close. "Ryan is going to hate me."

"Actually, he told us to have a good time and recommended a nice little B&B in Ojai."

"A good idea," she said. "We should get out of the house."

They'd gone out a few times for meals, but for the most part, they stayed in her place. Lounging by the pool, reading, talking. And even watching every Francesca Muratti movie made, to her complete frustration.

"I'd watch all of *Bright Eyes*," he'd told her, "but there are too many episodes. Saving that project for later."

"I need you to send me files for all of your projects. You know all about me from my movies. I need to learn all about you."

"Ah, there's where we differ. Confidential."

"Yeah? So if I was like a double-agent, I'd be trying to get the information from you in bed?" she'd teased. And then they'd ended up naked again. Which, as far as Simon was concerned, wasn't a bad thing at all.

When he took the official week of leave, though, they made more definitive plans. They went out into the world, exploring the stalls at the Rose Bowl Flea Market, visiting the observatory, taking the ferry to Catalina. He felt like a tourist again. And Frannie did, too. She kept her hair up and under a floppy hat, wore no make-up, and dressed in flowy, peasant-style dresses. He thought she looked incredible. And no one recognized her. Or, if they did, they realized she was incognito and didn't bother her.

That had been the idea—to let them go out together and have fun while keeping Frannie safe from prying eyes.

As far as the threat, the case had officially been closed with Frannie, Matthew, and Ryan all signing off on the decision. Burnet's mysterious shooter probably didn't exist at all. The simplest explanation was that Leslie had made up the story to help her defense. And the simplest solution was usually the right one.

But even if there was a mystery shooter, if they'd known that Frannie had been there that night, they would have dealt with her a long time ago. And if they'd only learned it because of Burnet's poking around, they most likely knew that Frannie didn't have any idea who the shooter was. All of which meant that officially, the case was over. Unofficially, Simon intended to watch her like a hawk. And he intended to keep watching her. She was his now. And he would keep her safe.

They were on the ferry back from Catalina when he saw the way she was looking at two young girls, probably ten or eleven, writing in their pink diaries and giggling as they whispered to each other.

"Was that you once?"

She shook her head, clearly distracted. "No."

"Frannie?"

She tilted her head up at him, but she seemed to be looking right through him.

"What? What is it?"

"Can we go home? I need to see something." She reached for his hand. "Please?"

"Of course."

As soon as the boat docked, they headed for the car. She said nothing, and he didn't push. Something was on her mind, and he could wait until she was ready to tell him about it.

When they got back to the house, she bolted to her bedroom. He followed, then found her half under the bed as she tugged out a flowered hat box. She lifted it onto the bed, then started pulling out spiral notebooks until she finally tugged out a pink cloth-covered book like the girls on the ferry had been giggling over.

"Carolyn's diary," she said, climbing on the bed and holding the pink book in her lap. She raised her brows, then patted the space beside her. And that one little gesture said more than a week of exceptional sex. They were together.

They were a team.

And he'd fallen in love.

He took a moment to savor the moment then hurried to climb up beside her. She started flipping pages, going slowly every few moments to read a passage and smile. But for the most part, she was on a mission, and she didn't stop until she reached a double page spread that was full of cramped writing interrupted only by a butterfly, a snake, and a calligraphy-style V.

"This," she said, pointing to where the snake bumped up against a butterfly made of two Ds, one the mirror image of the other. "That's what she wrote instead of saying Pruitt or stepfather. The snake is the S and the butterfly is for Dad. Stepdad. Right?"

"Got it."

"She does it in a few other places, too. I'm a picture of a fan with a little R on it. And her mom is a drawing of a mummy."

He couldn't help but smile. "Typical kid."

"Pretty much. But then there's this." She tapped the page, and he saw a capital V with a wavy line through it, like someone had crossed it with a calligraphy pen.

"It's a V," he said.

"Yeah, but in context, she's talking about a person. So I figure she had a crush on some guy. And that means that he's the most likely guy to have come by her room that night."

"Oh." He scooted back so he was leaning against the headboard. "That's a stretch."

"Do you have another idea?"

"I do. But you're not going to like it."

Her shoulders fell, and he could hear her exhale. "You think I should drop it because it's been years and I won't figure it out anyway?"

"You said it, not me."

She made a face. "I know. I should. But now that I know there was someone else there—"

"Assuming the mom was telling the truth. And that's a big assumption."

"Maybe," she said. "But—"

She was interrupted by her phone, and then sighed as she glanced at the screen. "Aaron," she said. "Work beckons." She hit the button to put it on speaker.

"Hey," she said. "What's up?"

"You alone?"

She put her finger to her lips. "Yup. Clean bill. My stalker was a Woodward or Bernstein wannabe reporter. I am no longer under surveillance by Stark's finest."

He laughed. "You sound like you're in a good mood."

"I am," she said, taking Simon's hand and pressing it to her breast. He raised a brow but didn't resist. This was a game he was more than willing to play.

"Listen, I was hoping you could come over tonight. I got some revisions back on *Spiraling*, and I wanted to go over them with you."

"Problem?"

"Just some character stuff before I call the writer with notes."

She glanced at him, and Simon nodded. He'd rather stay in bed with her, but this was her job. And he should probably swing by his place and get a change of clothes anyway.

"Okay," she told Aaron. "It's five now. I can be there by six."

"Perfect. See you then."

She ended the call, then turned to him. "Where will you be when I get back?"

"That depends. Where do you want me?"

"Right here," she said, then grinned and added, "And bonus points if you're naked."

"Sweetheart, I'm all about the bonus."

Chapter Eleven

I should have known better than to look at my phone while I was pumping gas, because the first thing I see is a brand-new article about me, dredging up that old lie about me getting drunk and passing out in a hot tub.

It's to be expected, though. Old articles and new gossip always surface when a new production is ramping up. So I suppose I should be flattered that the public is paying attention.

Although the idea that I would drink that much—or do drugs, which I do *not* do—really rubs me the wrong way. I should have challenged it back in the day, but Aaron thought that I should let it slide. I was coming off *Bright Eyes*, and it would do me good to lose my super clean-cut image.

I'd agreed. It seemed reasonable at the time. Now everyone just figures that goes with my party girl persona. But that's not the way I party, and I should never have given in.

The only saving grace is that Simon doesn't believe it. As far as I'm concerned, his opinion is the only one that matters.

I finish pumping the gas, and when I get back into the car, I'm smiling. Who cares about idiotic articles? I have Simon.

I have Simon.

Wild how fast the world can shift. Head-spinning, really. I imagine some folks don't trust things that happen too fast, but I've never been one for slow builds. I burst onto the film and television scene practically overnight. I bought my house on a whim and love it even after a decade. I met Carolyn by craft services one day and decided she would be my bestie. She still would be if she were alive.

I'd read *Spiraling* once and knew I had to star in it. More, I'm certain it's going to clean up in awards season.

And once I got over hating him for being an arrogant prick, I knew without any hesitation that Simon was the man for me.

Yeah, sometimes things don't have to be overthought.

Sometimes you just know. Sometimes things just are.

I'm thinking about life and sex and all that Simon-y stuff as I pull up at Aaron's place in the hills.

And, of course, as soon as I arrive, Simon falls out of my thoughts, and I'm back to being irritated about the damn article again.

"Don't let it worry you," Aaron says, leading me to the back porch. "We'll deal with it. If you want us to, we'll challenge it. The fact that you weren't even at this party should make a big difference. We can get people who were there to testify to that. But I still don't think it's worth the trouble."

"Fine. Whatever." Thinking about it is just going to piss me off. And I don't want to be in a pissy mood when we talk about the script. "But I want a drink."

He laughs. "I'm not surprised." He steps behind the outdoor bar and pulls open the wine fridge. "How about my famous wine cooler?"

"Perfect," I say. He mixes red wine with sparkling fruit juice, and it's like drinking heaven. "Did you want to work out here? Or are we going inside?"

"Hot tub okay? My back is killing me."

I shrug. This may not be the most traditional working environment, but Aaron and I have known each other since I was practically in diapers. Well, okay, I was ten and he was nineteen. So sitting in a hot tub getting a script all damp as we flip pages in the steaming water is not only a familiar setting, but a comfortable one.

"There should be a suit that fits you in the pool house. Go ahead. I'm already wearing trunks."

Sure enough, I find the pink two-piece I usually wear when I visit, and when I come back, he's set a nice large plastic cup filled with yummy nectar on the side of the hot tub.

I climb in, then take the copy of the script he hands me, careful not to get it wet. "How extensive are these notes?"

"Not bad. We'll be done in an hour. Maybe two."

"Good. Because I've been having a lovely week off with Simon. And I would like to get back to that as soon as possible."

He laughs. "Good. That first day at your house, I thought you might actually bite his head off. Now I guess there's a different type of biting going on."

"La la la, I don't kiss and tell."

"Since when?" he asks, and I make a face, then take a long sip of my cooler.

"We've come a long way, haven't we?"

"That's for sure," he says. "You know there's nothing I wouldn't do for you."

"The feeling is mutual."

"I'm really glad to hear that."

I frown, something in his voice making me uneasy. "Is there something going on? Nothing with *Spiraling,* is it?"

"No. It's nothing, really. Just some personal shit. Makes me glad to have a friend like you."

"Dating stuff?"

"Not exactly. Okay, maybe a bit."

I take his hand. He's not in the tub yet, just sitting on the side, with his feet in. "You need to get out there more. You used to date a lot. You stopped."

"I guess my heart hasn't been in it." He picks up his wine and holds it out for a toast. I tap my glass against his and take a large swallow.

The only trouble with this drink is how easy it goes down. Fortunately, I know that Aaron keeps a car service on call, so if I get too tipsy, it'll be easy to get home. Or I can always get my boyfriend to pick me up.

The thought makes me smile. *Boyfriend.*

Boyfriend.

Oh, sexy boyfriend.

I should have eaten more. Three big swallows and I'm already feeling loopy.

I take another sip as the hot tub starts to get warmer, then try to focus as Aaron goes through his notes, all of which I agree with, though I'm having a hard time focusing.

I close my eyes and lean back, feeling so incredibly relaxed. "This might have been a mistake," I say.

"What?"

"Working in the hot tub with drinks. I could just fall asleep right here."

"I'll turn down the temperature," he says, picking up his phone and going to the app that controls the pool. Instead of getting cooler, though, I feel the hot tub immediately start to get hotter.

"I think you hit the wrong button."

"Damn," he says, but nothing seems to change. I reach for my drink and finish it, then sigh. My eyes are starting to get very hard to hold open, and I'm feeling more dizzy than drunk. And heavy and exhausted.

"Aaron, I'm not feeling so good."

"Oh, sweetie, I'm so sorry."

"Think I'm gonna get out."

"Hold on," he says, "let me go get you a towel."

I start to protest, but I can't seem to form the words. I feel very strange. And something is very, very wrong. Really wrong. So wrong. But I don't know what it is that's wrong...

My eyes are drooping, and that's when I see it.

His fence.

The wrought iron that surrounds the property. There's a monogram mixed in about every ten feet. It's an open triangle crossed by a line at a slant with a slight curve at the end. The letter A. A is for Aaron.

I've seen that before.

Where have I seen that before?

I try to keep my eyes open so I can get a better look, but it's just not possible. My eyes close, and I feel myself start to slip. I try to push myself up, knowing that if I fall off this step, my head will be under water. But I'm sliding, and I can't seem to help myself.

The water is over my mouth, coming close to my nose. I want to cry out, but if I open my mouth, I'll breathe it in. I try to hold on to the side, but my fingers aren't working. And as the water starts to tickle my nose— as I try to force my feet to hold me steady and keep my head above the water—I realize where it is that I've seen that A before. But when I saw it, it was upside down. It was a V with a calligraphy line. V is for villain.

Oh, God.

The V in Carolyn's diary. It wasn't a V at all. It was an upside-down A.

Aaron was her mysterious boyfriend.

Aaron was the one who was there the night that she died.

Aaron saw me talking with the reporter at the con.

And now, Aaron is trying to kill me to protect his secret. Just like he killed Carolyn and her family when he thought that she'd betrayed him with her stepdad.

And as the water rises, sucking me under, the only thing I can think is that I'm going to die now. And Simon will never know just how desperately I was falling in love with him.

Chapter Twelve

He should have gone with her. That was the bottom line. For years, Simon had been living perfectly fine on his own. Now the woman he was falling in love with was gone for about forty-seven seconds, and he was already going batshit crazy.

He paced her living room, then saw the diary. He picked it up. They'd already gone over it in such detail, he doubted that he would see anything else, but the truth was he needed something to occupy his mind. He flipped pages, pausing at those odd Vs, wondering who it could be.

Frannie didn't remember anybody with a first or last name that started with a V, but memory wasn't always reliable. Maybe he should get on the *Bright Eyes* IMDB page and see if there was somebody in the crew whose name began with the letter V. He was seriously considering doing that when the phone rang, and he snapped it up the moment he saw it was Matthew.

"Hey, what's up?" he asked.

"I called Frannie, but she's not answering her cell. Is she with you? Ryan said you two were an item now. Congratulations. But I need a moment to run something by her."

"Sorry. I'm at her place, but she's out working on some project with Aaron."

"What new project?"

"*Spiraling.*"

"*Spiraling?* Are you sure?"

"All I know is what Aaron said. He wanted to go over some revision notes."

"That doesn't make sense," Matthew said.

"Why not?" Simon's entire body had gone tense.

"Because we haven't gotten the new pages yet. In fact, I talked to the writer not an hour ago, and she said that she'd have them tomorrow."

His blood felt like ice. "Maybe she got an advance read from Aaron before she runs them by you?"

"No. I've worked with this writer dozens of times. That would never happen."

"Why would he tell her that if it wasn't the case? Is there something else in the works?"

"A PR nightmare. Another damn article about that hot tub incident came out today," Matthew said. "But I can't see why that would require a meeting between the two of them."

Simon silently agreed. He glanced down and saw the diary sitting open. From his perspective now, it was upside down, and for a moment, that odd V looked like an A.

Oh, fuck.

"Matthew, did Aaron know Carolyn?"

"Carolyn Pruitt? Of course. They met on *Bright Eyes.*"

"Do you have his address?"

"What's going on?" Matthew asked after rattling it off.

"Something horrible. Just meet me there."

Twenty minutes later, Simon, Mario, Matthew, Trevor, Jasper, and Leah were all converging on Aaron's property.

"We're going in fast," Simon said as they coordinated by phone. "I called, but she didn't answer her phone. Something's going on. I don't know what it is, but I'm not waiting to find out. No politeness, just in and fast. Understood?"

They all assented, and the next thing he knew, they were at the house, each taking their particular entry point as Mario hacked in and disabled the security system.

Simon chose to go in through the back. He remembered what Matthew had said on the phone. About the hot tub article. Surely it wasn't a setup.

Except of course it was a setup, and the moment Simon was through the back gate, his entire body started to shake. She was there. In the hot tub. Her hair floating on the water. Her face completely submerged.

Oh God. Oh God. Oh God.

He didn't remember telling the others, but as Simon raced toward her, Jasper's voice rang out that an ambulance was on the way. Simon yanked her out by the underarms, scraping her back on the tile coping but not even caring. He laid her down flat and felt for a pulse. There wasn't one.

Damn it, damn it, damn it. The curse rattled through his head at the same time that the instructions for CPR filled his mind. *Compressions, breath, compressions, breath,* and all the while he was screaming and cursing. "Breathe, damn it, Frannie, breathe."

Again, and again, and again and then—oh, thank God—she coughed, turned her head to the side, and threw up a lake full of water.

"I'm here," he said, taking her hand as he crouched beside her.

Her eyes fluttered open. "Aaron," she said weakly. "My drink."

"I know, baby," he said as the chatter broke through his earpiece. Trevor had intercepted Aaron in the house, and he and Leah had taken him down. "I thought I'd lost you."

"I knew … you'd come." Her voice was weak. Thready. But she was alive, and the ambulance was on its way, along with cops who'd detain Aaron.

Then Aaron himself was there, struggling as Trevor and Leah led him, cuffed, onto the back porch.

"This is a mistake. I'd never hurt Frannie. I went into the house for a minute. Dammit, Frannie, with your history, you shouldn't drink in a hot tub."

"You son of a bitch," Simon said. "You tried to kill her. You did kill Leslie and Pruitt."

"What? What are you talking about? And no. Frannie was drunk. I must not have realized how drunk she was. I'm so sorry."

"Shut the fuck up," Trevor said, and then, in a move that had Simon silently applauding, he gave the bastard a shove, and Aaron fell hard onto his knees. He'd have one hell of a limp as he maneuvered prison, and Simon couldn't help but smile.

He rode in the ambulance with Frannie, holding her hand all the way, his pulse so fast he thought he would pass out from fear. She had to be fine. She'd talked to him, she'd smiled at him. So she had to be fine, but he couldn't completely believe it, not until two different doctors had told him that she was okay. She'd barely slipped under when he'd arrived. She hadn't lost oxygen to the brain long enough to cause any damage.

He was crying when he was finally allowed to go to her bedside after she was admitted for observation overnight. "I'm staying with you," he said. "I'm staying right here all night."

"Good," she said. "Thank you."

"You're mine, Frannie. I'm not letting go of you. Not now, not ever.

If you want out of this, out of whatever we have, you're going to have to fight your way out. Because I'm hanging on tight. You almost died tonight, and it almost killed me, too. I'm in love with you. I am absolutely certain of it. And this is going to last. It's going to work."

"Then I guess you better kiss me," she said, her voice still raw from choking on the water. "Don't you know that's how all the best stories end?"

Epilogue

I stand on the platform with Matthew on one side of me and Simon on the other, my hand tight in his. We've already been past the step and repeat, but still the cameras are flashing as the crowd of reporters and photographers gather around us.

Matthew steps forward, holding the mic. "Thank you so much for coming to our wrap party for *Spiraling*. I loved this script from the first moment Frannie showed it to me, and I think it's appropriate now that I turn the stage over to her."

I squeeze Simon's hand, then look out at the crowd. Over the years, I've come to recognize most members of the press, so their faces all look familiar, and it's easy to smile. Why not? This incredible film is wrapped, I'm alive, and Simon's hand is warm and comforting in mine.

"I really just wanted to thank you for coming. I'm so excited for this project. As you all know, there were some stumbling blocks after Freeway Flix changed ownership, but I owe Matthew and Hardline Entertainment a debt of gratitude for keeping the project alive. I'm happy to answer any questions about the film you might have, but I would like to reiterate that I won't be talking about Aaron Kepner, Freeway Flix, or anything related to *Bright Eyes*."

Beside me, Simon tightens his grip, and I appreciate it. As he well knows, I've spent countless hours talking to the police and giving interviews about my relationship with Carolyn and Aaron. Thankfully, my lawyer has already made clear to the press that I can't talk about his attempt to kill me. But that doesn't mean I can't feel the topic bubbling in the air.

In front of me, a dozen hands shoot up, and I point to John, one of the reporters I've known for over a decade. "We understand you have some personal news. Care to give us an official statement?"

I glance sideways at Simon, who takes a step forward. "I'm pretty sure she asked for questions regarding the movie."

"Oh, come on, Simon," John says. "You both know what we're all waiting for."

"Fine, fine," Simon says, then turns to me with that gorgeous smile. "Go ahead, baby. The press wants a story, right?"

The reporters all laugh, and more cameras snap as I flash my most camera-ready smile.

"Fair enough. I know you're all expecting an engagement announcement. I'm sorry to tell you there won't be one."

I keep a straight face as I watch the reporters squirm.

"But—" John begins.

"Instead, I'd like to officially introduce you all to my husband, Simon Barré."

There's a moment of confused silence, then a burst of applause that rises even higher when Simon pulls me close and kisses me. When it finally dies down, he takes the mic. "We got married last weekend," he says. "In Tahoe. And if you'd like a statement from me, you can tell the world that I'm the luckiest man alive."

"Yeah," I say with a tease, "you really are." Then I tug on his tie to pull him back to me and kiss him hard as cameras snap, video rolls, and applause thunders around us.

Because honestly, how perfect is that?

Pretty damn perfect, at least as far as I'm concerned. And considering the congrats after we step off the platform, I think the rest of the crowd agrees with us.

Zelda Clayton is the first to give me a hug. Her brown hair hangs in waves around her face, and she looks younger than her twenty-four years. We met a few weeks ago at her birthday party, thrown by our mutual friend Jamie Archer Hunter, who's not only Ryan's wife but is starring in the adaptation of one of Zelda's books.

"I'm so excited for you. Huge congratulations."

"You, too," I say. "When are you and Jasper tying the knot?"

She glances down at her engagement ring, then smiles up at me. "A few more months. We're planning the wedding around the honeymoon. Paris first, then Rome."

"Good for you," I say, and we both laugh.

I'm about to ask where Jasper is, but I see him walking with Damien and Trevor. He peels off, then steps up and hooks his arm around Zelda's waist. She leans against him, looking for all the world like the two of them have been together always.

"What's up with Trevor and Mr. Stark?" she asks her fiancé. "They look so serious."

"I overheard something earlier," Jasper tells us. "The FBI wants Trevor to come on board for one of their operations."

"Really?" Simon's brow rises. "Will he be working with Ollie McKee?"

Jasper nods. "Apparently, it's his project, and he asked specifically for Trevor."

"Interesting," Simon says, sharing a knowing look with Jasper.

"What?" I ask. "Why?"

Zelda rolls her eyes. "Because Trevor's gay, and Ollie's not. That we know of. But Trevor has a crush. Plus, I've heard from Jamie that she's started to speculate that Ollie might be bi. And since Jamie's one of Ollie's oldest friends..." She trails off with a shrug.

"Hey, they're solid friends," Jasper says. "If they end up being more than that, then good for them."

I look at Simon. "Whatever happens, I hope they're as happy as we are."

"Amen to that," he says, then seals the words with a kiss.

The End

Did you miss Jasper and Zelda's story? You can find it here!

And don't miss Trevor and Ollie in Tangled with You, coming from 1001 Dark Nights in 2023.

Finally, be sure to subscribe to my newsletter so you're among the first to know when the next Stark Security book is available for pre-order!

* * * *

Also from 1001 Dark Nights and J. Kenner, discover Memories of You, Cherish Me, Tease Me, Indulge Me, Damien, Hold Me, Tame Me, Tempt Me, Justify Me, Caress of Darkness, Caress of Pleasure, and Rising Storm.

Sign up for the 1001 Dark Nights Newsletter
and be entered to win a Tiffany Key necklace.

There's a contest every month!

Go to www.1001DarkNights.com to subscribe.

**As a bonus, all subscribers can download
FIVE FREE exclusive books!**

Discover 1001 Dark Nights Collection Nine

DRAGON UNBOUND by Donna Grant
A Dragon Kings Novella

NOTHING BUT INK by Carrie Ann Ryan
A Montgomery Ink: Fort Collins Novella

THE MASTERMIND by Dylan Allen
A Rivers Wilde Novella

JUST ONE WISH by Carly Phillips
A Kingston Family Novella

BEHIND CLOSED DOORS by Skye Warren
A Rochester Novella

GOSSAMER IN THE DARKNESS by Kristen Ashley
A Fantasyland Novella

DELIGHTED by Lexi Blake
A Masters and Mercenaries Novella

THE GRAVESIDE BAR AND GRILL by Darynda Jones
A Charley Davidson Novella

THE ANTI-FAN AND THE IDOL by Rachel Van Dyken
A My Summer In Seoul Novella

CHARMED BY YOU by J. Kenner
A Stark Security Novella

THE CLOSE-UP by Kennedy Ryan
A Hollywood Renaissance Novella

HIDE AND SEEK by Laura Kaye
A Blasphemy Novella

DESCEND TO DARKNESS by Heather Graham
A Krewe of Hunters Novella

BOND OF PASSION by Larissa Ione
A Demonica Novella

JUST WHAT I NEEDED by Kylie Scott
A Stage Dive Novella

THE SCRAMBLE by Kristen Proby
A Single in Seattle Novella

Also from Blue Box Press

THE BAIT by C.W. Gortner and M.J. Rose

THE FASHION ORPHANS by Randy Susan Meyers and M.J. Rose

TAKING THE LEAP by Kristen Ashley
A River Rain Novel

SAPPHIRE SUNSET by Christopher Rice writing as C. Travis Rice
A Sapphire Cove Novel

THE WAR OF TWO QUEENS by Jennifer L. Armentrout
A Blood and Ash Novel

THE MURDERS AT FLEAT HOUSE by Lucinda Riley

THE HEIST by C.W. Gortner and M.J. Rose

SAPPHIRE SPRING by Christopher Rice writing as C. Travis Rice
A Sapphire Cove Novel

MAKING THE MATCH by Kristen Ashley
A River Rain Novel

A LIGHT IN THE FLAME by Jennifer L. Armentrout
A Flesh and Fire Novel

Discover More J. Kenner

Memories of You: A Stark Security Novella

Hollywood consultant Renly Cooper is fed up with relationships. His recent breakup with a leading lady played out across the tabloids, and the former Navy Seal is more than ready to focus on his new position as an agent at the elite Stark Security agency. He's expecting international stakes. Instead, his first assignment is to protect one of Damien Stark's friends from a stalker. A woman who, to his delight, turns out to be one of his closest childhood friends.

After a foray into online dating puts tech genius Abby Jones in danger, she needs a bodyguard, and her business partner, Nikki Fairchild Stark, enlists help from Stark Security. When the assigned agent turns out to be her best friend from junior high—and her first crush—she's thrilled to discover he's even more delicious now. She hopes one sexy night can turn into more, but Renly is firmly in the friends-with-benefits camp.

As the threat to Abby increases, she tries to keep her growing feelings for Renly at bay. But as the sparks between them burn even hotter, can they go from friends to lovers when the first order of business is simply to keep Abby alive?

* * * *

Cherish Me: A Stark Ever After Novella

My life with Damien has always been magical, and never more so than during the holidays, a time for us to celebrate the hardships we've overcome and the incredible gift that is our family. Over the years, he has both protected and cherished me. He has made my life more rich and full than I could ever have imagined.

This year, he's treating me and our daughters to a holiday in Manhattan. With parades and ice skating, toy displays and candies. And, most of all, with each other.

It's a wonderful gift, a trip I will always cherish. But this year, I'm the one with the surprise. And I can't wait to see the look of delight and awe when I finally share my secret with Damien.

But I'm terrified that when danger strikes, it will take a holiday miracle for me to even get the chance.

* * * *

Tease Me: A Stark International Novel

Entertainment reporter Jamie Archer knew it would be hard when her husband, Stark Security Chief Ryan Hunter, was called away for a long-term project in London. The distance is difficult to endure, but Jamie trusts the deep and passionate love that has always burned between them. At least until a mysterious woman from Ryan's past shows up at his doorstep, her very presence threatening to destroy everything that Jamie holds dear.

Ryan never expected to see Felicia Randall again, a woman with whom he shared a dark past and a dangerous secret. The first and only woman he ever truly failed.

Desperate and on the run, Felicia's come to plead for his help. But while Ryan knows that helping her is the only way to heal old wounds, he also knows that the mission will not only endanger the life of the woman he holds most dear, but will brutally test the deep trust that binds Jamie and Ryan together.

* * * *

Indulge Me: A Stark Ever After Novella

Despite everything I have suffered, I never truly understood darkness until my family was in danger. Those desperate hours came close to breaking both Damien and me, but together we found the strength to survive and hold our family together.

Even so, my wounds are deep and wispy shadows still linger. But Damien is my rock. My hero against the dark and violence.

When dark memories threaten to consume me, he whisks me away, knowing that in order to conquer my fears he must take control. Demand my submission. Claim me completely. Because if I am going to find my center again, I must hold tight to Damien and draw deep from the spring of our shared passion.

* * * *

Damien: A Stark Novel

I am Damien Stark. From the outside, I have a perfect life. A billionaire with a beautiful family. But if you could see inside my head, you'd know I'm as f-ed up as a person can be. Now more than ever.

I'm driven, relentless, and successful, but all of that means nothing without my wife and daughters. They're my entire world, and I failed them. Now I can barely look at them without drowning in an abyss of self-recrimination.

Only one thing keeps me sane—losing myself in my wife's silken caresses where I can pour all my pain into the one thing I know I can give her. Pleasure.

But the threats against my family are real, and I won't let anything happen to them ever again. I'll do whatever it takes to keep them safe—pay any price, embrace any darkness. They are mine.

I am Damien Stark. Do you want to see inside my head? Careful what you wish for.

* * * *

Hold Me: A Stark Ever After Novella

My life with Damien has never been fuller. Every day is a miracle, and every night I lose myself in the oasis of his arms.

But there are new challenges, too. Our families. Our careers. And new responsibilities that test us with unrelenting, unexpected trials.

I know we will survive—we have to. Because I cannot live without Damien by my side. But sometimes the darkness seems overwhelming, and I am terrified that the day will come when Damien cannot bring the light. And I will have to find the strength inside myself to find my way back into his arms.

* * * *

Justify Me: A Stark International/Masters and Mercenaries Novella

McKay-Taggart operative Riley Blade has no intention of returning to Los Angeles after his brief stint as a consultant on mega-star Lyle Tarpin's latest action flick. Not even for Natasha Black, Tarpin's sexy personal assistant who'd gotten under his skin. Why would he, when Tasha made it absolutely clear that—attraction or not—she wasn't interested in a fling, much less a relationship.

But when Riley learns that someone is stalking her, he races to her side. Determined to not only protect her, but to convince her that—no matter what has hurt her in the past—he's not only going to fight for her, he's going to win her heart. Forever.

* * * *

Tame Me: A Stark International Novella

Aspiring actress Jamie Archer is on the run. From herself. From her wild child ways. From the screwed up life that she left behind in Los Angeles. And, most of all, from Ryan Hunter—the first man who has the potential to break through her defenses to see the dark fears and secrets she hides.

Stark International Security Chief Ryan Hunter knows only one thing for sure—he wants Jamie. Wants to hold her, make love to her, possess her, and claim her. Wants to do whatever it takes to make her his.

But after one night of bliss, Jamie bolts. And now it's up to Ryan to not only bring her back, but to convince her that she's running away from the best thing that ever happened to her--him.

* * * *

Tempt Me: A Stark International Novella

Sometimes passion has a price...

When sexy Stark Security Chief Ryan Hunter whisks his girlfriend Jamie Archer away for a passionate, romance-filled weekend so he can finally pop the question, he's certain that the answer will be an enthusiastic yes. So when Jamie tries to avoid the conversation, hiding her fears of commitment and change under a blanket of wild sensuality and decadent playtime in bed, Ryan is more determined than ever to convince Jamie that they belong together.

Knowing there's no halfway with this woman, Ryan gives her an ultimatum – marry him or walk away. Now Jamie is forced to face her deepest insecurities or risk destroying the best thing in her life. And it will take all of her strength, and all of Ryan's love, to keep her right where she belongs…

* * * *

Caress of Darkness: A Dark Pleasures Novella

From the first moment I saw him, I knew that Rainer Engel was like no other man. Dangerously sexy and darkly mysterious, he both enticed me and terrified me.

I wanted to run—to fight against the heat that was building between us—but there was nowhere to go. I needed his help as much as I needed his touch. And so help me, I knew that I would do anything he asked in order to have both.

But even as our passion burned hot, the secrets in Raine's past reached out to destroy us … and we would both have to make the greatest sacrifice to find a love that would last forever.

Don't miss the next novellas in the Dark Pleasures series!

Find Me in Darkness, Find Me in Pleasure, Find Me in Passion, Caress of Pleasure…

* * * *

Storm, Texas.

Where passion runs hot, desire runs deep, and secrets have the power to destroy…

Nestled among rolling hills and painted with vibrant wildflowers, the bucolic town of Storm, Texas, seems like nothing short of perfection.

But there are secrets beneath the facade. Dark secrets. Powerful secrets. The kind that can destroy lives and tear families apart. The kind that can cut through a town like a tempest, leaving jealousy and destruction in its wake, along with shattered hopes and broken dreams. All it takes is one little thing to shatter that polish.

Rising Storm is a series conceived by Julie Kenner and Dee Davis to read like an on-going drama. Set in a small Texas town, Rising Storm is full of scandal, deceit, romance, passion, and secrets. Lots of secrets.

About J. Kenner

J. Kenner (aka Julie Kenner) is the *New York Times*, *USA Today*, *Publishers Weekly*, *Wall Street Journal* and #1 International bestselling author of over one-hundred novels, novellas and short stories in a variety of genres.

JK has been praised by *Publishers Weekly* as an author with a "flair for dialogue and eccentric characterizations" and by *RT Bookclub* for having "cornered the market on sinfully attractive, dominant antiheroes and the women who swoon for them."

In her previous career as an attorney, JK worked as a lawyer in Southern California and Texas. She currently lives in Central Texas, with her husband, two daughters, and two rather spastic cats.

Visit JK online at www.jkenner.com
Subscribe to JK's Newsletter
Text JKenner to 21000 to subscribe to JK's text alerts
Twitter
Instagram
Facebook Page
Facebook Fan Group

Discover 1001 Dark Nights

COLLECTION ONE
FOREVER WICKED by Shayla Black ~ CRIMSON TWILIGHT by
Heather Graham ~ CAPTURED IN SURRENDER by Liliana Hart ~
SILENT BITE: A SCANGUARDS WEDDING by Tina Folsom ~
DUNGEON GAMES by Lexi Blake ~ AZAGOTH by Larissa Ione ~
NEED YOU NOW by Lisa Renee Jones ~ SHOW ME, BABY by
Cherise Sinclair~ ROPED IN by Lorelei James ~ TEMPTED BY
MIDNIGHT by Lara Adrian ~ THE FLAME by Christopher Rice ~
CARESS OF DARKNESS by Julie Kenner

COLLECTION TWO
WICKED WOLF by Carrie Ann Ryan ~ WHEN IRISH EYES ARE
HAUNTING by Heather Graham ~ EASY WITH YOU by Kristen
Proby ~ MASTER OF FREEDOM by Cherise Sinclair ~ CARESS OF
PLEASURE by Julie Kenner ~ ADORED by Lexi Blake ~ HADES by
Larissa Ione ~ RAVAGED by Elisabeth Naughton ~ DREAM OF YOU
by Jennifer L. Armentrout ~ STRIPPED DOWN by Lorelei James ~
RAGE/KILLIAN by Alexandra Ivy/Laura Wright ~ DRAGON KING
by Donna Grant ~ PURE WICKED by Shayla Black ~ HARD AS
STEEL by Laura Kaye ~ STROKE OF MIDNIGHT by Lara Adrian ~
ALL HALLOWS EVE by Heather Graham ~ KISS THE FLAME by
Christopher Rice~ DARING HER LOVE by Melissa Foster ~ TEASED
by Rebecca Zanetti ~ THE PROMISE OF SURRENDER by Liliana
Hart

COLLECTION THREE
HIDDEN INK by Carrie Ann Ryan ~ BLOOD ON THE BAYOU by
Heather Graham ~ SEARCHING FOR MINE by Jennifer Probst ~
DANCE OF DESIRE by Christopher Rice ~ ROUGH RHYTHM by
Tessa Bailey ~ DEVOTED by Lexi Blake ~ Z by Larissa Ione ~
FALLING UNDER YOU by Laurelin Paige ~ EASY FOR KEEPS by
Kristen Proby ~ UNCHAINED by Elisabeth Naughton ~ HARD TO
SERVE by Laura Kaye ~ DRAGON FEVER by Donna Grant ~
KAYDEN/SIMON by Alexandra Ivy/Laura Wright ~ STRUNG UP by
Lorelei James ~ MIDNIGHT UNTAMED by Lara Adrian ~ TRICKED
by Rebecca Zanetti ~ DIRTY WICKED by Shayla Black ~ THE ONLY
ONE by Lauren Blakely ~ SWEET SURRENDER by Liliana Hart

COLLECTION FOUR
ROCK CHICK REAWAKENING by Kristen Ashley ~ ADORING
INK by Carrie Ann Ryan ~ SWEET RIVALRY by K. Bromberg ~
SHADE'S LADY by Joanna Wylde ~ RAZR by Larissa Ione ~
ARRANGED by Lexi Blake ~ TANGLED by Rebecca Zanetti ~
HOLD ME by J. Kenner ~ SOMEHOW, SOME WAY by Jennifer
Probst ~ TOO CLOSE TO CALL by Tessa Bailey ~ HUNTED by
Elisabeth Naughton ~ EYES ON YOU by Laura Kaye ~ BLADE by
Alexandra Ivy/Laura Wright ~ DRAGON BURN by Donna Grant ~
TRIPPED OUT by Lorelei James ~ STUD FINDER by Lauren Blakely
~ MIDNIGHT UNLEASHED by Lara Adrian ~ HALLOW BE THE
HAUNT by Heather Graham ~ DIRTY FILTHY FIX by Laurelin Paige
~ THE BED MATE by Kendall Ryan ~ NIGHT GAMES by CD Reiss
~ NO RESERVATIONS by Kristen Proby ~ DAWN OF
SURRENDER by Liliana Hart

COLLECTION FIVE
BLAZE ERUPTING by Rebecca Zanetti ~ ROUGH RIDE by Kristen
Ashley ~ HAWKYN by Larissa Ione ~ RIDE DIRTY by Laura Kaye ~
ROME'S CHANCE by Joanna Wylde ~ THE MARRIAGE
ARRANGEMENT by Jennifer Probst ~ SURRENDER by Elisabeth
Naughton ~ INKED NIGHTS by Carrie Ann Ryan ~ ENVY by Rachel
Van Dyken ~ PROTECTED by Lexi Blake ~ THE PRINCE by Jennifer
L. Armentrout ~ PLEASE ME by J. Kenner ~ WOUND TIGHT by
Lorelei James ~ STRONG by Kylie Scott ~ DRAGON NIGHT by
Donna Grant ~ TEMPTING BROOKE by Kristen Proby ~
HAUNTED BE THE HOLIDAYS by Heather Graham ~ CONTROL
by K. Bromberg ~ HUNKY HEARTBREAKER by Kendall Ryan ~
THE DARKEST CAPTIVE by Gena Showalter

COLLECTION SIX
DRAGON CLAIMED by Donna Grant ~ ASHES TO INK by Carrie
Ann Ryan ~ ENSNARED by Elisabeth Naughton ~ EVERMORE by
Corinne Michaels ~ VENGEANCE by Rebecca Zanetti ~ ELI'S
TRIUMPH by Joanna Wylde ~ CIPHER by Larissa Ione ~ RESCUING
MACIE by Susan Stoker ~ ENCHANTED by Lexi Blake ~ TAKE THE
BRIDE by Carly Phillips ~ INDULGE ME by J. Kenner ~ THE KING
by Jennifer L. Armentrout ~ QUIET MAN by Kristen Ashley ~
ABANDON by Rachel Van Dyken ~ THE OPEN DOOR by Laurelin

Paige~ CLOSER by Kylie Scott ~ SOMETHING JUST LIKE THIS by Jennifer Probst ~ BLOOD NIGHT by Heather Graham ~ TWIST OF FATE by Jill Shalvis ~ MORE THAN PLEASURE YOU by Shayla Black ~ WONDER WITH ME by Kristen Proby ~ THE DARKEST ASSASSIN by Gena Showalter

COLLECTION SEVEN
THE BISHOP by Skye Warren ~ TAKEN WITH YOU by Carrie Ann Ryan ~ DRAGON LOST by Donna Grant ~ SEXY LOVE by Carly Phillips ~ PROVOKE by Rachel Van Dyken ~ RAFE by Sawyer Bennett ~ THE NAUGHTY PRINCESS by Claire Contreras ~ THE GRAVEYARD SHIFT by Darynda Jones ~ CHARMED by Lexi Blake ~ SACRIFICE OF DARKNESS by Alexandra Ivy ~ THE QUEEN by Jen Armentrout ~ BEGIN AGAIN by Jennifer Probst ~ VIXEN by Rebecca Zanetti ~ SLASH by Laurelin Paige ~ THE DEAD HEAT OF SUMMER by Heather Graham ~ WILD FIRE by Kristen Ashley ~ MORE THAN PROTECT YOU by Shayla Black ~ LOVE SONG by Kylie Scott ~ CHERISH ME by J. Kenner ~ SHINE WITH ME by Kristen Proby

COLLECTION EIGHT
DRAGON REVEALED by Donna Grant ~ CAPTURED IN INK by Carrie Ann Ryan ~ SECURING JANE by Susan Stoker ~ WILD WIND by Kristen Ashley ~ DARE TO TEASE by Carly Phillips ~ VAMPIRE by Rebecca Zanetti ~ MAFIA KING by Rachel Van Dyken ~ THE GRAVEDIGGER'S SON by Darynda Jones ~ FINALE by Skye Warren ~ MEMORIES OF YOU by J. Kenner ~ SLAYED BY DARKNESS by Alexandra Ivy ~ TREASURED by Lexi Blake ~ THE DAREDEVIL by Dylan Allen ~ BOND OF DESTINY by Larissa Ione ~ MORE THAN POSSESS YOU by Shayla Black ~ HAUNTED HOUSE by Heather Graham ~ MAN FOR ME by Laurelin Paige ~ THE RHYTHM METHOD by Kylie Scott ~ JONAH BENNETT by Tijan ~ CHANGE WITH ME by Kristen Proby ~ THE DARKEST DESTINY by Gena Showalter

Discover Blue Box Press
TAME ME by J. Kenner ~ TEMPT ME by J. Kenner ~ DAMIEN by J. Kenner ~ TEASE ME by J. Kenner ~ REAPER by Larissa Ione ~ THE SURRENDER GATE by Christopher Rice ~ SERVICING THE TARGET by Cherise Sinclair ~ THE LAKE OF LEARNING by Steve

Berry and M.J. Rose ~ THE MUSEUM OF MYSTERIES by Steve Berry and M.J. Rose ~ TEASE ME by J. Kenner ~ FROM BLOOD AND ASH by Jennifer L. Armentrout ~ QUEEN MOVE by Kennedy Ryan ~ THE HOUSE OF LONG AGO by Steve Berry and M.J. Rose ~ THE BUTTERFLY ROOM by Lucinda Riley ~ A KINGDOM OF FLESH AND FIRE by Jennifer L. Armentrout ~ THE LAST TIARA by M.J. Rose ~ THE CROWN OF GILDED BONES by Jennifer L. Armentrout ~ THE MISSING SISTER by Lucinda Riley ~ THE END OF FOREVER by Steve Berry and M.J. Rose ~ THE STEAL by C. W. Gortner and M.J. Rose ~ CHASING SERENITY by Kristen Ashley ~ A SHADOW IN THE EMBER by Jennifer L. Armentrout

On Behalf of 1001 Dark Nights,

Liz Berry, M.J. Rose, and Jillian Stein would like to thank ~

Steve Berry
Doug Scofield
Benjamin Stein
Kim Guidroz
Social Butterfly PR
Asha Hossain
Chris Graham
Chelle Olson
Kasi Alexander
Jessica Saunders
Dylan Stockton
Kate Boggs
Richard Blake
and Simon Lipskar

Made in the USA
Middletown, DE
05 August 2022